THE HIDDEN

BLACK FORCE SHORTS BOOK FOUR

MATT ROGERS

Join the Reader's Group and get a free 200-page book by Matt Rogers!

Sign up for a free copy of '**HARD IMPACT**'.
Meet Jason King — another member of Black Force.

Experience King's most dangerous mission — action-packed insanity in the heart of the Amazon Rainforest.

No spam guaranteed.

Just click here.

BOOKS BY MATT ROGERS

THE JASON KING SERIES

Isolated (Book 1)

Imprisoned (Book 2)

Reloaded (Book 3)

Betrayed (Book 4)

Corrupted (Book 5)

Hunted (Book 6)

THE JASON KING FILES

Cartel (Book 1)

Warrior (Book 2)

Savages (Book 3)

THE WILL SLATER SERIES

Wolf (Book 1)

Lion (Book 2)

BLACK FORCE SHORTS

The Victor (Book 1)

The Chimera (Book 2)

The Tribe (Book 3)

The Hidden (Book 4)

Visit amazon.com/author/mattrogers23 and press **"Follow"** to be automatically notified of my future releases.

1

W ill Slater took one look through the entranceway to the cocktail lounge and figured, at twenty-three years of age, he probably didn't mesh with the typical Friday night crowd. Mood lighting covered the interior in a dark hue, and the soft jazz filtering through the air had a relaxing undercurrent. Not the sort of scene a man who should be fresh out of college would eagerly dive into.

Then again, he was not a normal twenty-three year old.

So he stepped across the threshold without a second thought, exchanging a brief nod with the broad-shouldered bouncer manning the door. The guy didn't even think about asking for identification, and Slater hadn't expected him to. Something about working for a black operations division of the U.S. military charged him with a confidence that couldn't be faked. He kept his chin held high and his shoulders back. It hadn't even crossed the bouncer's mind that Slater could be underage.

Slater certainly didn't look twenty-three.

The last six months of his life had consisted of such

utter madness, such indescribable carnage with no end in sight, that he felt right at home mingling with an over-whelmingly older crowd. Any kind of social awkwardness or hesitation had been rudely stripped away. Slater had come to embrace the strangeness of life, and in the brief periods of downtime he'd received over the last half-year he'd thrown himself in the deep end, seizing every opportunity that came his way, even if it made him uncomfortable.

So he had no qualms about approaching the two women sitting across from each other on bar stools in the far corner of the room.

No-one glanced at him twice as he made his way through the lounge. He passed broad leather armchairs arranged stylistically in tight groups, most of them occupied by wealthier types. This was a socialite's haven, which explained the attractiveness of the women by the bar. They appeared to be the only people in the room roughly similar to Slater in age. He put them at no older than twenty-five. Strangely enough, it took him a moment to realise that he was probably wealthier than half the people in this room, even though most of them were three times his age.

Black operations paid handsomely and offered impres-sive rewards if you survived the job.

Which was no easy task.

Slater opted to ignore the nagging aches and pains in his body from the last three consecutive operations. Neverthe-less, he took them as a sign of achievement. He shouldn't have survived any of the situations he'd found himself in.

Which added confidence to his psyche.

Which seeped through into his abilities.

Which made him a better soldier.

The effect of compounding.

If he strode into a situation without a shadow of a doubt

that he would succeed, the sheer mental edge often swayed results in his favour. The battlefield had taught him that. But he was starting to learn that it also applied to almost anything in life.

Namely, most social encounters...

Slater stopped alongside the two women and rested both elbows on the countertop, an enormous slab of polished wood with accompanying downlighting to accentuate the shadows of the giant bar. He was in shape, and he didn't feel the need to hide it. Men in this cocktail lounge had probably spent thousands of dollars on designer clothes to hide their flabby physiques and the fat running around their mid-sections. The benefit of putting yourself through a fitness regime that most Olympic athletes would frown at, Slater had realised, was being able to dress in a twenty-dollar long-sleeved shirt and attract as much attention as one desired.

He noticed the women studying him out of the corner of his eye as he ordered a glass of eighteen-year-old Macallan, on the rocks.

'That'll be fifty dollars,' the bartender warned.

'Think I would have ordered it if I didn't know that?' he snapped.

'Just checking.'

'Fair enough.'

As the bartender set to work making the beverage, Slater figured he'd overreacted and made a mental note to correct the situation. When the man passed the drink across, Slater slid him seventy dollars cash with a knowing nod. The guy smiled, nodded back, and pocketed the change.

Strangely enough, Slater found himself stunned that he'd been so curt in the first place. It had been an astonishing six months, a whirlwind of solo operations — three missions, back to back to back — that had pushed him to his physical and mental limits. Each time he'd crawled out of the pit of war with his body barely held together. Each time he'd been patched back up and returned to the fray.

Hence his presence in Chicago.

He needed a break.

He needed rest and recuperation and some semblance of peace for a couple of weeks if he was going to do this job for the rest of his life.

Which he fully intended to do.

So he didn't even hesitate in turning to the pair of women and flashing a grin of pearly white teeth. Thankfully, although he'd been beaten to a pulp in every other way, he'd kept the workings of his mouth flawless. He assumed fake teeth would come in future if he maintained his current pace. He'd take it all in stride. Just as he'd handled everything in the last half-year.

'Hi,' he said. 'Figured I'd introduce myself. Will Slater.'

He shook each of their hands in turn, applying just enough firm pressure to let them know he meant business. The woman closest to him seemed to be the elder of the two, although she couldn't have been more than a couple of years older than Slater. Physically, she was stunning — model calibre at the very least, with an expensive black dress hanging off a slender frame and a long flowing mane of golden hair. The other woman was a redhead, slightly shorter with a more curvaceous physique. She seemed in impeccable shape — Slater figured she lifted weights religiously. He found that even more attractive.

'You're forward, aren't you?' the taller of the pair said.

Slater eyed the empty cocktail glass on the countertop in front of her and noticed the warm glint in her eyes. She'd had a couple of drinks to take the edge off.

He shrugged. 'I think we're the only people in here under the age of fifty.'

They both laughed.

'Bit of an exaggeration,' the redhead said.

Slater cast a quick look over his shoulder. 'Not really.'

'What are you doing here, then?' the taller one said. 'If it's not your crowd.'

'Did I say it wasn't my crowd?'

'You seem to think we shouldn't be here.'

'You're both single?' Slater said.

'Cutting right to the chase, aren't you?' the redhead said, but she was grinning devilishly.

'Well,' Slater said, sensing his opportunity, 'I just figured — why else would you be here?'

'We're both single.'

'Looking for a guy with money?'

'You're not supposed to say things like that to people you've only just met.'

Slater leant in, and neither of the pair flinched or shrank away. He took that as a positive sign. By now he was only half a foot from the taller woman, and he downed half his Macallan. Before continuing, he flashed a look into the woman's eyes, and she met his gaze. Her eyes were stark green, piercing, vibrating with energy. She sensed something there.

So did he.

'I mean, there's no point skirting around it, is there?' he said. 'I can't see anyone in this room who would give you a fun time. They might buy you nice things down the road, but where's the fun in that? I'm young. I'm single. You could wait around here all night in the hope of striking up a shit conversation with one of these grumpy old bastards, or the three of us could stick together.'

'Stick together?' the redhead said, raising an eyebrow.

'How about I buy you a drink? Let's talk.'

'Thanks for the offer, but—'

'Why not?' Slater said, fixing his attention on the taller model.

She returned the stare, in much the same way she had before. There was palpable chemistry there, two young beautiful souls free in Chicago for a night. That concept had electricity — it had potential. She could sense that. Slater certainly could.

The redhead wasn't buying it.

'I'm going to the bathroom,' she muttered. 'Florence...'

The taller woman — Florence, evidently — twisted around, a sly smile edging at the corners of her mouth. She gave her companion a quizzical glance.

'Bathroom,' the redhead repeated.

Slater knew what was happening. The redhead expected Florence to accompany her, at which point they would be free to gossip about the overly forward, well built African-American man in the bar who neither of them had any intention of taking home. If she went, Slater had lost her, and he might as well be on his way. In that brief moment in time he subtly applauded himself for having the courage to approach someone so stunning, so exquisite. Florence seemed to be captivated by it, too — maybe her beauty put men off cold approaching her.

He'd certainly taken a risk.

Florence nodded to her friend. 'No problem. I'll be here.'

Slater stifled a grin, keeping his expression deadpan.

The redhead silently huffed, trying to make a scene as best she could without drawing attention to it, and shifted off the bar stool. She disappeared into the corner of the cocktail lounge in search of the facilities.

Slater hunched forward another few inches.

Now they were overtly close.

Close enough for both their intentions to be placed on the table. Slater could smell her perfume.

'I have to say,' he muttered, taking another sip of the Macallan. 'Your friend doesn't seem very fun.'

Florence eyed the drink. Slater took the cue and handed it over — she drained the rest of the eighteen year old scotch in a single gulp.

'Where to?' she whispered.

Slater smiled.

2

S later had stepped inside the cocktail lounge at just after nine in the evening.

It was past midnight when Florence rolled off him and sprawled across the other side of the king size bed, sweat glistening off her naked body, her chest rising and falling as she panted for breath. Slater considered himself in peak physical condition, but the preceding hours had tested his endurance all the same.

The lighting in the penthouse suite had been deliberately set to low, creating an almost romantic aura as the pair covered themselves with the crumpled bedsheet. Slater lifted an arm and Florence dropped her head to his chest, kissing his bare skin softly at random intervals. They lay there for some time, savouring the shared state of bliss, staring out over the Chicago River and the skyline running along the opposite bank.

The room had cost Slater two thousand for the night, but money had become the least of his worries six long months ago.

'So...' Florence muttered, tracing a bare finger across his

chest, pressing down in random places, admiring his frame, 'I don't think we ever discussed who we are.'

'That's a pretty broad question,' Slater said.

'I mean, career-wise.'

'Oh.'

'You don't want to talk about it?'

Slater paused. 'I mean... I could lie. But I came here to get away from all that bullshit. I'd rather tell the truth, but I can't. So I'll just say nothing.'

'You could have made up anything.'

'I know. I'm a little tired, though.'

'I can't imagine why.'

'You do this kind of thing often?'

'You mean... for three hours?'

Slater masked a smirk. 'No. Strangers. People you've never met before.'

'Not usually.'

'Then why me?'

'There was something about you.'

'Oh?'

'The fact that you can't tell me what you do. I like that. That whole aura. You had it when you walked into the bar tonight.'

'Newfound confidence, I guess.'

'From what?'

'What life throws at me.'

'Do you like what life throws at you?'

'No.'

'But you still do it.'

'I do.'

'Why?'

Slater swept a hand around the room. 'You know... the usual. It buys things like this.'

Florence shook her head, planting another delicate kiss on his left pectoral. 'No, no. You're not that kind of guy.'

'You're a good judge of character...'

'I know.'

Slater shrugged. 'You don't have to enjoy something to know it's what you're supposed to do.'

She visibly clenched her teeth. 'You're really not going to tell me, are you?'

'I don't change my mind often. I'm pretty stubborn.'

'I could return... favours.'

'I don't think I've got the stamina for the kind of favours you have in mind.'

'You've got plenty of stamina. I'm sure you'll survive.'

'Afraid I can't talk. Lips are sealed.'

'That's a shame.'

Slater looped his hand around the small of her back and ran a finger down the base of her spine, bringing a soft flutter to her lips.

'And what about you?' he said.

'What about me?'

'What do you do?'

'This and that.'

'I think I know what that means.'

She raised an eyebrow. 'Careful. I'm not a hooker, for God's sakes.'

'I never said you were.'

'But?'

'But there's something there. In your eyes. Some kind of spark. You do things your own way. You make money from that, don't you?'

She shrugged and offered a flirtatious smirk. 'There's always opportunities out there.'

'Big businessmen who need a companion? That sort of thing?'

'I've only ever done it twice.'

Slater believed her. Not that he would have cared either way. He wouldn't be back in Chicago for a long time. 'Only twice?'

'You seem to think I'm a slut.'

'Not at all. But if I were in your shoes -- if I had your looks — I'd use them.'

Florence trailed a hand down his abdomen, and it came to rest in a sensitive area. She pressed her lips to the side of his neck, then came away and whispered, 'You could probably use them now.'

'Twice,' he muttered. 'Why'd you stop?'

She shifted uncomfortably. 'None of your business.'

'You don't want to talk about it. So it's important. Whatever it is.'

'Your secrets seem important, too.'

Slater sensed something there, a piece of information he was desperate to know. He relented. 'Let's compromise. A fair trade.'

'A trade?'

'You tell me what you're hiding. And I'll tell you what I do.'

'Do you do awful things?'

'Define that.'

'Do I want to know?'

'You won't hate me.'

'I can live with that.'

'You first, then,' he said.

She shrugged. 'I... saw something. And I'm the only person who knows about it.'

'To do with the businessman?'

She nodded. 'The second guy. He's the CEO of a property law firm. I won't name him.'

'He's got dark secrets?'

'Yes... well, I assume. But it's not what you might think.'

'Oh?'

'I was sleeping with him. About a month ago. It helped that he was attractive, and somewhere around thirty. I like a guy with ambition. But he had a wife, and a kid. So I was already uncomfortable off the bat.'

'And?'

'And they disappeared.'

'What?'

'The wife and kid. For a full week. They vanished.'

'How did you know?'

'He kept avoiding my calls — and, look, I don't know, I thought we had something. I was dumb. I thought it might have been more than just a fling. So I kept trying to contact him. And trying. And trying. And finally he picks up the phone and he's in a mad panic, and he tells me his family's been kidnapped. He just unloads it, like it had been on his mind for days and he finally had to release it. Then he realises he's made a mistake and hangs up. And I never hear from him again. The next week I pass him in downtown Chicago, and his wife and kid are right there. Like nothing happened at all. No press about it. Nothing.'

Slater took a moment to process the information. 'That *is* odd.'

'Now can you tell me what you do?' Florence said. 'Look — I probably shouldn't have just told you that. You need to keep quiet about it. Please. Oh, God, I hardly know you...'

He could sense the panic starting to set in. That information must have been weighing on her mind for some time, and Slater kissed her on the forehead to calm her down.

Despite his ability to keep up the facade of a hardened exterior, inwardly something stewed. He didn't like the story one bit, not for any obvious reason — six months into a black operations career, he had seen things up close that would ensure he never squirmed at gory details ever again — but because its mere presence hit him like a gut punch.

There was a reason it had ended up on his doorstep.

Florence had clammed up, sealing her lips before sharing any other sensitive details, but Slater had a grimy feeling he wasn't done with it. The circumstances were too odd, the coincidence too great...

Then the phone on the bedside table buzzed once, indicating an incoming call.

Only one man had access to that number.

Slater grimaced as he realised his vacation in Chicago might not involve as much recuperation as he might have thought.

'You want my secret?' he muttered in Florence's ear.

She nodded.

'I kill people for the government,' he said, and got straight to his feet. He shouldn't have told her, but he figured she deserved to know.

But the simple act of sharing that information meant he now had to vanish.

He slid into the same jeans and long-sleeved cotton shirt, both still brand new, and snatched the smartphone off the bedside table. Without a second glance back at the bed, he quickly checked the room for any stray possessions and, finding none, hurried straight out into the hotel corridor before Florence could utter a word of protest.

Never to return.

3

He didn't bother checking the caller ID, because he knew the number would be blocked. He stepped into the plush hotel hallway with nothing but the clothes on his back, his phone, and his wallet — the only possessions he'd ventured to Chicago with. When his clothes got dirty he would buy new ones, and then after a week or so of aimless wandering he would return to active service, where all his material needs would be met. He had never been a man of materialistic tendencies, and he didn't think he ever would be. He preferred the raw, sensual experiences.

He guessed that made him a hedonist.

Judging by his actions over the past few hours, he wasn't ready to protest the label.

He answered the call and pressed the phone to his ear as he called for the elevator. 'Lars.'

'How'd you know it was me?' the man said.

'Who the hell else would be calling me?'

Lars Crawford handled Black Force operatives. He was the only member of the shadowy organisation that Slater had met in the flesh — the equivalent of a human relations manager for an army of solo warriors. Slater hadn't been acquainted with any of the other Black Force operatives — Lars tirelessly drilled home the concept of the division, highlighting the fact that operatives and officials interacting with each other would ruin the deniability of the organisation.

Slater didn't care either way.

He was content with being paid millions to put his life on the line for his country.

And even though he'd knocked on death's door several times over his short career, he didn't see any signs of slowing down in the immediate future.

Hence the lack of possessions, and the spontaneous trip to Chicago, and the three-hour romp with a model he'd just met.

He was a man of impulse, and he embraced it with open arms.

'How's the vacation?' Lars said.

'It's okay. I've got my feet up.'

'I'm sure you do,' Lars said, with all the scorn of a man who knew Slater's personality inside and out.

'What's that supposed to mean?'

'I don't think you've put your feet up in three years, apart from when you need sleep. And you don't need sleep often.'

'You know me too well.'

'I do. Which is why I'm calling.'

Slater stepped into an empty cable car and rode it down to the hotel lobby, praying the call didn't cut out in the metal box. Thankfully, the hotel had employed counter-measures to prevent that, and the reception held.

He breathed a sigh of frustration. 'You need me?'

'I do.'

'Is it urgent?'

'It's unique.'

'Everything I do for you is unique.'

'Which is why you're necessary. You'll be paid.'

'It's not about the money.'

'It should be. Our organisation's breaking records with our payouts.'

'That's because everything is off the books, Lars,' Slater said, as if scolding a child. 'You can afford to throw millions at us. Besides, when we die you can just take it straight back.'

'You're awfully cynical tonight.'

Slater thought of what Florence had told him. 'Just got a bad vibe about Chicago.'

'Hate to break it to you, but that vibe's about to get a whole lot worse.'

Slater sighed. 'Thought you might say that.'

'How long will you need to get ready?'

As if on cue, the elevator doors slid silently open and Slater strode straight across the lobby. He didn't stop at the reception desk, manned even at this hour by the receptionist working the night shift. He'd prepaid upon booking the penthouse suite, in case he needed to make a hasty departure for any number of reasons. He'd made sure that no check-out was required.

He despised lingering in one place any longer than necessary.

The grand entranceway led out onto the esplanade, running parallel to the Chicago River. From there, a world of opportunity awaited. Slater could head in any direction he wanted, young and healthy and rich.

In his prime.

Except he was tethered by binding contract to whatever Lars Crawford instructed him to do.

He would probably be indebted to the U.S. government for the rest of his life, considering his recklessness and lack of ability to read the fine print. He'd signed the contracts without scrutinising them — in truth, Black Force could have swindled him.

But he never thought anything through.

He simply bounced from one bout of madness to the next, in whichever form that took. Somehow, it had led him here, building him into one of the pioneers of a division breaking new ground in the realm of reflexes and reaction time.

At least, that's what he was told.

So as he stepped out into a chilly Chicago night and swept his gaze over the river, he took a deep breath and responded with, 'Ready now.'

'Good,' Lars said.

Without hesitation.

As if he'd expected nothing less.

'Where do you need me?'

'I need you to get yourself arrested,' Lars said.

'What?'

'You heard me.'

4

'Head west,' Lars said. 'Away from the coast.'

Slater spun in a tight circle, flashing dark looks at every civilian in the immediate vicinity. Finding nothing suspicious, he turned back to face the river and hissed into the phone, 'Do you have eyes on me?'

'No. But I can track that phone.'

'Black Force doesn't watch me on my time off, do they?' Slater said. 'Because I wouldn't like that one bit.'

'You're a twenty-three year old kid,' Lars said, turning stern. 'You don't get to tell us what you do and don't like. You signed your life away, in case you forgot.'

'I didn't sign it away. You're paying me millions. And in your own words, I'm "one of the rawest talents you've ever seen?"'

'Don't get cocky, kid.'

'All I'm saying is that you need me.'

'No,' Lars said. 'We don't watch you. But you seem awfully sensitive about it. I'm guessing you had a female companion.'

'I can do what I want in my downtime.'

'I never said you couldn't. But this isn't downtime anymore. You're officially back on active duty.'

'There's nothing official about this,' Slater muttered, lowering his voice.

'West,' Lars said. 'Walk.'

Slater set off at a measured pace, struggling to soak in the beauty of Chicago's nightlife. The stroll along the esplanade offered stunning views of the skyline, with the skyscraper lights making the still water shimmer in the gloom. It was cold, but not cold enough to be uncomfortable. Slater loosened up as he quickened his pace, heading fast in a streamlined direction. The whole time, he kept the phone pressed to his ear.

'You going to tell me what this is about?' Slater said.

'A Commander in the Chicago Police Department.'

'Name?'

'Ray D'Agostino.'

'Sounds like a lovely man,' Slater said, his tone dripping with sarcasm.

'He's in charge of the Central District. Runs it with an iron fist, by all accounts. Good for the books. His arrest rates are solid. Pulls in all manner of vagrants.'

'Not seeing any red flags so far.'

'Three homeless men he brought into custody for public intoxication have died in their cells in the last two weeks.'

'That happens.'

'Not with that frequency. And not under suspicious circumstances. And not all under the jurisdiction of a single commander. That's a lot of red flags right there.'

Slater sensed frustration brewing. He'd been secretly hoping for some downtime, whatever that entailed. His relentless approach to life had served him well for the better part of four years now, but everyone had their limits. Chicago had been an uncharacteristic request, but Lars had granted it, knowing full well what Slater had been through over the course of his first three operations. The fact that he was being yanked back into the line of fire for something like this set his blood boiling.

'This isn't our fucking problem, Lars,' he hissed. 'Isn't that for internal affairs? Or the FBI? Or whoever the hell runs that kind of thing?'

'We need to employ discretion.'

'But still... how is this my problem? What do you want me to do? Rough him up and get him to confess to being a sociopath who gets off on killing vagrants? Is that what you want?'

'No,' Lars said.

Slater grew quiet. He knew when his handler turned to single syllables, shit was milliseconds away from hitting the fan. He reminded himself of the fact that, by all accounts, he was still classified as a reckless youth as far as black operations were considered. He'd only been whisked into the program because of another operative — something Lars had been hesitant to divulge, but had eventually shared with Slater. A man by the name of Jason King, one year younger than Slater, who was shattering the myths that elite operatives needed to be in their thirties.

The two misfits, Slater thought.

He wondered if he would ever meet Jason King.

Then his mind wandered back to the present.

'Look, Lars,' he said. 'I just don't get it. I really needed this time off. Hopefully you can understand.'

'And we equally need you now,' Lars said. 'What do you think I do all day? Sit around and masturbate and wait for something to slide across my desk that I can throw to one of my operatives?'

'Uhh...'

'Everything is vetted and analysed and scrutinised and picked apart. You should be aware that if something gets passed onto you, it's of the utmost importance. You've been deemed the best fit for this operation for a number of reasons, and I don't have time to lay them all out. That's not my job, and it's not your job to know. You just need to follow through with it. Okay?'

'Okay.'

'I'm going to give you directions to a construction site. The entire block was abandoned months ago — the building company went into liquidation. The area's a hotspot for vagrants and squatters, and I need you to go there and make a scene. D'Agostino patrols that area excessively, even though it's not his job. If it's not him, then it's one of his men. They'll bring you in, and you'll try your best to figure out what his deal is, or if he's involved. I don't want to give you any more than that, because I trust you to improvise and do your job. Got it?'

'Got it.'

'You know any government forces that have the capacity to act like a homeless man, and kill if necessary?'

'No.'

'That's why we need you. You don't exist. Remember that.'

'So if it goes belly up in there, I'm on my own?'

'That's always been the deal. Surely you're not getting second thoughts about that now.'

'But I have full discretion?' Slater said. 'This is an ordinary job in all respects, right?'

'Of course. If D'Agostino tries to kill you, you can fight back. But if you're going to use physical force, make sure you have a way to get the hell out of there. We can't come in and save you in a hurry.'

'The three guys. How'd they die?'

'Two from intoxication. There was enough alcohol in their bloodstream to kill a horse. But the autopsies are... sketchy, to say the least. It didn't help that D'Agostino made it as difficult as he could to properly study the bodies. There's marks on both their necks. Like they were held down.'

'And the third?'

'Stabbed by a fellow cellmate.'

'Who?'

'No-one knows. Cameras were off at the time.'

'That's some pretty serious shit to go down in a holding cell. Is the district investigating?'

'D'Agostino doesn't seem like he's in a hurry to crack down on it.'

'Sounds like a real slimy piece of shit.'

'Good. Hopefully that motivates you to get the job done.'

'Could be a coincidence.'

'Could be. You'll find out.'

'This is sketchy, Lars.'

'So is everything you do for us. Since when has that ever stopped you?'

'Get myself arrested. Act suspicious. See if D'Agostino has a crack at me. Find out why. Break out of the station. Anything else?'

'That should just about do it.'

'You owe me.'

'If D'Agostino's bent, and we find out why, and we nail him for it, I'll give you a million.'

'You really do have a fat purse, don't you?'

'I wasn't lying the first time we met. The best work

deserves the best rewards. Especially if you maintain a consistent track record.'

'I don't exactly have time to spend it,' Slater said.

'Saving for retirement,' Lars said, and Slater could sense the sheer sarcasm in his voice.

'Retirement sounds an awful lot like dying in my early twenties in this field.'

'If you make it out the other side,' Lars said, 'you'll have some wild stories to tell.'

'You bet I will.'

'I'll forward you the address. Good luck, kid. Go to work.'

The line disconnected and Slater slid the phone back into the pocket of his jeans. He shoved his hands in his pockets and quickened his stride, pounding pavement to mitigate his nerves.

Twenty-three years old.

At this pace he wasn't sure he'd make it to see twenty-four.

5

The GPS co-ordinates came through in a text message a couple of minutes later. Slater stared at them, memorised them, burned the numbers and decimals into his mind. Sure enough, a moment later the message vanished off his phone, as if it had never existed at all.

Which it hadn't.

And neither did he.

He continued along the esplanade for close to a mile before branching off into the central district. At this hour — well past midnight — all the businesses were closed, and the sidewalks were largely devoid of life. Slater passed an assortment of shifty characters as he powered through the streets, but there was enough purpose in his stride and confidence in his demeanour to ward off any potential muggings.

In fact, he almost welcomed a brazen attack.

It wouldn't end well for whoever opted to approach.

He employed the same detailed strategy as the rest of

the operations he'd undertaken for Black Force — he simply forced the finer details from his mind and relied on sheer momentum.

It had worked well for him so far.

He hoped it held such unbelievable results in future.

Although something told him it would put him in a shallow grave.

The construction site was unmistakable — Slater spotted the half-finished skyscraper immediately, awkwardly slotted into an enormous stretch of land between two shiny new buildings. He checked his phone, unsurprised that Lars had made no further attempts to contact him. Over the course of their shaky history, a rapport had been established between the two men that suited Slater just fine. He hadn't fit into the traditional military structure — in fact, Lars revealed that Slater had been days away from a dishonourable discharge before Black Force made their offer.

Slater had talent — there was no doubt about that.

But he worked best when the situation walked the fine line between right and wrong, the morally grey area that black operatives needed to live in. Their work was suppressed, their existence denied, and that suited Slater just fine.

Grateful that he wasn't decked out in designer clothing — it would be hard to pass himself off as a vagrant otherwise — Slater stepped up onto the barren sidewalk in front of the construction site and set to work ruining his appearance. He stood in the lee of the enormous building, dwarfed by rusting scaffolding and metal walkways twisting skyward in an urban amalgamation of steel. It seemed like no-one had stepped foot in the structure in years. The entire skyscraper lay shrouded in darkness, its edges barely illuminated by the weak street lights.

Slater hefted a jagged piece of metal off the ground and stabbed holes in his clothing at random, taking care not to cut himself at risk of succumbing to a cocktail of infectious diseases.

Then it became a waiting game, something he considered himself adept at. He tossed the piece of metal back to the ground and scooped a heap of gravel and dust into his palm, wiping it over his face to convey a certain look. He always kept his hair in a simple buzzcut, but if it had been grown out he would have tussled it up.

Many of the details concerning Ray D'Agostino and his involvement in something sinister were a mystery to Slater, but that was the way he preferred it. If Slater was to act like a homeless beggar in the hopes of getting arrested, he would rather be kept in the dark, allowing himself to make things up on the fly. If every part of the operation had been planned in painstaking detail, it wouldn't have meshed with Slater's natural tendencies.

Lars had come to learn that over their brief shared history, so now his handler let him do what he wanted.

Which, in this case, consisted of planting himself down in the dirt and leaning back against a partly finished brick wall. He let his head fall back against the scratchy surface, and there he waited.

In full view of pedestrians and passing traffic.

There wasn't much to look at.

The occasional vehicle trundled past, but none seemed to take any interest whatsoever in the vagrant sprawled out across the sidewalk. Slater imagined there were thousands of similar sights across Chicago — homelessness was not a rarity in this city. He kept still and made sure to break out in drunken mumbling whenever a pedestrian ambled by, which didn't happen often. On the rare occurrences that it did, the passersby made a beeline across the street to avoid him.

The minutes blurred into hours, and Slater felt right at home. He could wait all night, if that was what it took. In the field an operative sees what he's truly made of, and Slater had come to learn that he could put himself through almost anything if he had a clear goal in mind.

Right now, it was to find out whatever the hell D'Agostino's deal was.

So when he spotted the first patrol vehicle after at least two hours of inactivity, he made sure to roar an obscenity at the police car and flip two middle fingers in its direction. It crawled slowly past, its windows tinted and its pace measured, sporting the insignia of the Chicago Police Department on the side of the sedan.

Surprisingly, it didn't stop.

Slater settled back into a seated position as the patrol car disappeared into the night.

Odd, he thought.

Ninety nine times out of one hundred, that would have kicked up enough of a fuss to warrant an arrest, especially considering the stereotype he was portraying. It didn't take much in this day and age.

Slater stewed silently, annoyed that he hadn't been able to capitalise on such a wide opening. But if he had proven anything to himself over the last six months, it was his unwavering stubbornness. So he stayed sprawled across the sidewalk, overshadowed by the enormous construction site behind him. He would wait days, if that was what it took. Surely another patrol car would approach within the next few hours.

Then, not twenty minutes later, he heard a screaming siren in the distance, approaching fast.

Making a beeline toward his position.

He sat up and realised the initial patrol car hadn't stopped for a reason.

6

T his was D'Agostino's area.

 Whatever that meant.

 Whatever that implied.

Slater pieced it all together in an instant, even before the Chicago P.D. sedan screamed around the corner, its lights sending blue and red waves across the surrounding buildings. The street was a ghost town — the cops had picked the perfect time to make the arrest if they had sinister intentions. There wasn't a passing pedestrian or civilian vehicle in sight.

No witnesses.

If it was D'Agostino, then all Slater's suspicious would be confirmed.

Slater briefly thought about the fact that he still had his phone in his pocket. He had ample opportunity to discard it, simply turning around and throwing it into the bowels of the construction site, but there was nothing damaging on the device. It had been sealed with military-grade encryption, and all the data that Slater processed from Lars was wiped off the phone within two minutes of receiving it. And in this era, it was perfectly acceptable for a homeless man to carry a cellphone. They were considered more important than housing to some.

So he kept the phone in his pocket and tucked his knees to his chest, waiting for the police sedan to screech to a halt across the sidewalk in front of him.

Which was exactly what happened.

A man leapt out of the passenger's seat even before the vehicle had come to a standstill. His black jacket hung over a muscular frame — the guy had good genetics, but it seemed he'd combined that with a solid workout regime.

It was D'Agostino, alright.

The guy was Italian, in his late thirties with a sturdy jawline and short, close-cropped jet black hair. He moved with athleticism as he crossed from the sedan to the pavement in front of Slater. As he moved, Slater realised there was something else there.

Something more than simple agility.

This guy was moving like a man possessed.

Like a man caught in the act.

But what act?

Why was he so desperate to yank homeless men off the streets in this exact location?

Slater figured he'd find out soon enough.

'What's up, brother?' Slater said, louder than he should have, taking the time to stumble on his words.

D'Agostino said nothing. He bent down, wrapped a powerful hand around the back of Slater's neck, and hauled him to his feet. Slater figured he could have broken twelve bones in the space of three seconds if he so desired, but he had a role to play, and that role involved drunkenness and carelessness.

So he allowed himself to be manhandled.

For now.

D'Agostino shoved him hard in the back, pinning his chest against the brick wall. Slater grunted and played up his outrage. 'Whoa! What's this for? Get off me, man. What the hell is this?'

'Shut the fuck up,' D'Agostino snarled.

'That doesn't sound like the Miranda rights.'

Slater had been expecting the use of unnecessary force, but not quite to the extent of what followed. D'Agostino utilised his strength to shove an elbow into the back of Slater's neck, sending him face first into the wall. The *crack* that followed sunk through his brain, delivering a staggering bolt of agony along with it. Slater paused in time, making sure to keep his feet underneath him even though his knees grew weak. The pain was horrendous, but it peaked at the initial break. When the blood started to flow out of his nose, he brought himself back under control.

For a terrifying moment, he'd almost lost control of his restraint.

Then there would have been a body in the street, and an entire district of cops seeking justice for their commander.

'You think any of that matters?' D'Agostino spat. 'Look at you.'

'Not cool, man,' Slater mumbled through bloody lips, even though he wanted to do a whole lot more than talk.

But the operation trumped everything else. So he stood quiet, shoulders slumped so D'Agostino couldn't get a proper look at his physique. The big commander yanked Slater's arms behind his back and fastened them together with steel handcuffs, clamping down a couple of extra notches to cause maximum discomfort.

Slater squirmed, but said nothing.

'What am I under arrest for?' he said, trying not to spit

blood over D'Agostino as the man turned him around to face him.

'Whatever I say you're under arrest for.'

'I'm just trying to sleep out here, man.'

'Wrong place to sleep.'

'Why?'

D'Agostino said nothing. His face had turned to stone. He hauled Slater across the sidewalk and shoved him into the back of the squad car. The passenger — an unimpressive small white man in his early thirties with a badge on his uniform — opened the rear door to receive Slater. As Slater stumbled past him, the guy stared at the ground, refusing to make eye contact.

Implicit in the abuse, but unwilling to say anything.

No spine, Slater thought as D'Agostino crammed him into the seat.

He didn't need to play along for D'Agostino to haul him around. The commander had serious strength — Slater wondered if he was a recreational powerlifter — and he yanked Slater left and right with ease. The commander slammed the door on Slater and the pair of cops slotted back into their places — D'Agostino in the passenger's seat, the other guy in the driver's.

Slater wondered how long it would take them to get back to the station.

As the sedan peeled off the sidewalk, Slater let the blood from his broken nose flow over his cotton shirt. The garment had already been ruined, but the crimson wave added insult to injury. He watched D'Agostino like a hawk — even though the sedan's cabin lay shrouded in darkness, enough of a glow from the streetlights filtered in to make out the commander's facial features.

D'Agostino didn't take his eyes off the unfinished skyscraper as the sedan accelerated down the street.

Only when they rounded the corner did he turn his attention back to the road ahead.

Slater masked a wry smile.

Police brutality was an issue, but not something a Black Force agent was ordinarily tasked with investigating. But police brutality in order to hide something darker...

Slater remembered the way D'Agostino had acted around the construction site.

Like an addict protecting his stash.

Got you, you bastard, Slater thought.

He gave himself the mental permission to use force if the situation required it, and then he sat back and waited for the madness to ensue.

7

Alone with his thoughts in the back of the sedan, separated from D'Agostino and his partner by a mesh screen, Slater had time to piece together what had happened.

He ignored the throbbing in his nose, even when the pain drilled up through his brain and intensified behind his eyeballs. He'd suffered all manner of grievous injuries before, and this was just another broken bone to compartmentalise and deal with later. His eyes were watering, but he ignored it. He focused on what he could control.

The initial patrol car had spotted him. At first he'd thought they'd foolishly passed him by, but D'Agostino must have specifically requested to be notified of any vagrants hanging around that area. It was something to do with the construction site — Slater was sure of it. The pace at which D'Agostino had hauled him off the sidewalk and put him in handcuffs wasn't a normal response to a squatter. Slater hadn't even done anything inherently hostile — not yet, anyway.

He would give D'Agostino reason to fight back soon.

By then it would be too late for the police commander to do anything anyway.

But he needed more information. Either through provoking the man, or striking up an innocent conversation that managed to whittle out some more details. Slater didn't figure D'Agostino would let anything incriminating slip out, so option number one seemed to be the best choice.

Piss him off.

'You sure pulled me in quick, man,' he mumbled through the metal screen. 'Almost like you got something to hide, hey? What are you hiding, brother?'

He conveyed the ramblings like that of a mindless drunk, but he wondered if D'Agostino would jump at the accusation.

Sure enough, the commander twisted in his seat and pushed the barrel of his Glock semi-automatic sidearm against a gap in the screen. 'One more word out of you...'

Slater feigned terror. 'Hey! Relax, buddy. Relax.'

'I told you to shut up.'

'You can't kill me, you know? That ain't legal.'

D'Agostino glanced across at his partner and laughed, an attempt at a mocking display, but it wasn't genuine. Slater saw right through it, saw the panic suppressed behind the man's eyes. D'Agostino was playing the bad cop, but he wasn't doing it because he wanted to. He was doing it to distract from something else.

Something his partner didn't know about, it seemed.

The other cop would turn a blind eye to D'Agostino's over-the-top measures, but he didn't know the reasons for them.

Slater didn't either, but he knew the commander was cleansing the construction site of vagrants.

D'Agostino probably didn't want anyone sniffing around that area.

Has the other cop clued into that yet?

Slater decided to test his luck.

'What's a big time commander like you doing out here, boss?' he said. 'This doesn't seem like your job, man. Why you so interested in me for?'

D'Agostino sent the Glock's barrel straight back in the same direction, pointed at Slater's head again. He didn't mind. He'd had weapons pointed at him before. He doubted the commander would do it in the sedan. Too messy. Too much clean-up.

And, even though he'd dished out some violence in front of his partner, Slater didn't think D'Agostino was ready to kill someone in front of the man. He would do it later, when the station was quiet and attention had died down.

Slater would be ready for it.

'Point that thing at me all you want,' Slater said. 'It's not scaring me, buddy. As a matter of fact my friend got picked up from that exact place a week ago. One of my old squatting pals. You know what happened to him? I been lookin' for him.'

Once again, he laced the drunken outpour with an undercurrent of truth. He was hoping for a visceral reaction, for D'Agostino to order his partner to stop the car and haul Slater out into the middle of the street, demanding the truth about what he knew.

But none of that happened.

D'Agostino kept his head screwed on straight, and even though his eyes burned with fury he twisted away from Slater, passing the rambling off as delusional.

'Bums,' he said to his partner. 'Fuckin' useless, the lot of them.'

Despite his best efforts, D'Agostino was unable to hide the rage in his voice. It boiled under the surface, threatening to burst out in the sedan. Slater hoped the man could keep it contained until they got to the station.

He was prepared for whatever would follow.

8

The blood had formed clots in Slater's nostrils by the time the police cruiser rumbled back into the station.

He sat still and patient with his hands squashed into the small of his back, pinned together by the biting cuffs. The circulation in his wrists had been cut off, so he squirmed from side to side in an attempt to alleviate the pain.

He channelled the pain into motivation.

Everything D'Agostino had done to him, he would use to propel him forward.

And a semblance of a plan was beginning to form in the back of his mind.

There was no doubt that D'Agostino was involved in something. Suspicion had turned to certainty, at least in Slater's opinion. The simple act of sitting on the sidewalk outside the construction site had resulted in being hauled off to the station with a broken nose. A completely unnecessary display of force, all carried out by a police commander in charge of an entire district who shouldn't have been tasked with making arrests like that in the first place.

Slater knew what was up.

D'Agostino had instructed any patrol car that spotted loiterers by that particular construction site to contact him immediately. He might have disguised it under the veil of orders from his superiors, but he was paying careful attention to that unfinished skyscraper.

There was something in there...

And he was keeping it a secret. Slater could tell by the way he puffed his chest out, pumping himself full of false bravado, as if pulling vagrants off the streets was the most noble cause in existence. All to distract from the fact that he didn't want someone stepping within a foot of that construction site.

And he didn't want his partner to know that was the reason.

So when the driver pulled the police cruiser to a halt in front of the station's side entrance and disappeared off down the footpath, Slater kept a close eye on D'Agostino. The man slipped out of the passenger seat, glanced in both directions with intense focus, and then skirted around to the rear door.

To Slater's door.

Slater was in no position to fight back. With his wrists cuffed, there was little he could do to protest. So he kept up the drunken act, gazing into the distance and letting his shoulders slump as D'Agostino pulled him out of the car. He got his feet underneath him and grimaced as the rapid motion sent a stab of pain through his shattered nose.

That would need medical attention as soon as he got out of this mess.

Interestingly, he noted that he might have underestimated the police commander. A quick look at his surroundings revealed an empty parking lot, cordoned off from the street by a tall wire fence, populated sparsely by a handful of official Chicago P.D. vehicles. The station itself was a long low building with a white brick exterior, its perimeter illuminated by harsh LED floodlights. Without a soul in sight, D'Agostino would be free to kill Slater here and pretend his body never existed.

But Slater's eyes wandered to the security cameras covering every inch of the concrete expanse, and figured D'Agostino was unwilling to make that bold of a move.

He was right.

D'Agostino eyed the cameras and grunted his frustration, confirming Slater's suspicious that the commander wanted him out of the picture.

The hairs on the back of Slater's neck rose. A certain dynamic unfolded when you knew someone wanted you in the ground. Slater stood inches away from the man, sensing his trepidation.

D'Agostino shoved a hand into the small of Slater's back and hurried him into the station through a side door.

9

The atmosphere shifted.

At the beginning of the night, Slater hadn't been fully convinced that D'Agostino was corrupt. Angry at Lars for interfering with his personal life, he'd spent most of the time loitering outside the construction site running through a list of reasons why the vagrants' deaths could be chalked up to simple coincidence. But now, after having met Ray D'Agostino in the flesh, and quietly observing how the man behaved, Slater knew he would have to see this through to its bloody conclusion.

Because D'Agostino wanted him dead for what he'd said in the car, and the man wasn't bothering to hide it anymore.

The commander led him through sterile white-washed corridors that probably stank of disinfectant — not that Slater could smell anything. They passed no other officers — either the station was sparsely populated at this time of the evening, or D'Agostino had deliberately headed down a deserted stretch of the building.

Slater imagined it was the latter.

At any point, he expected the big commander to make a

lunge for him. The Glock sidearm was still in its holster at D'Agostino's waist as he led Slater through the building, but the man made no attempt to snatch for it. Slater imagined he would need a damn good reason for firing on a vagrant in restraints.

He was biding his time.

And Slater could see it was eating the man alive.

They pulled up to a row of single-man holding cells and D'Agostino unlocked the door to the closest one, shoving Slater inside the tiny concrete box.

Slater turned as D'Agostino slammed the cell door closed — they were now separated by the metal bars.

Last chance, Slater thought. *Send a message.*

'I know what you're doing at that construction site,' he said, his voice suddenly sober, his drunken rambling ceased. 'How many more of us are you going to kill before you get busted, big man?'

D'Agostino froze in his tracks, his eyes flaring with surprise. Slater could almost see his mind racing behind his pupils, analysing just how much trouble he was in.

Not much, D'Agostino must have concluded. *If I can shut this guy up forever.*

Slater eyed the corridor outside the cell and found a single surveillance camera in the far corner, but there was no flashing digital light underneath the lens.

It wasn't rolling.

'Going to try and kill me, too?' Slater said. 'Come on in. Still got these cuffs on but I'll put up a fight. How you going to explain that?'

D'Agostino remained resolutely quiet.

Big guy, Slater could see him thinking. *Well-built. Strong frame. He'll be trickier to handle.*

'You're going in the drunk tank,' D'Agostino said.

'The drunk tank?'

Wordlessly, the commander unlocked the cell again and pulled Slater back out into the corridor. He led him down another set of hallways, darting this way and that, energy in his stride.

Nervous energy.

'What was wrong with that cell?' Slater grumbled.

'Shut up.'

'I know what you're doing at the construction site.'

'No idea what the hell you're talking about, kid.'

But D'Agostino wasn't even bothering to maintain any semblance of believability. His cheeks had turned pale, and the bravado he'd been holding himself with had dissipated. Slater figured the other vagrants he'd killed may have only hinted at seeing something in the construction site. Slater had not only confessed to being in the know; he'd actively tried to antagonise D'Agostino.

That must have thrown the man through a loop.

They pulled to a halt a minute later in front of a cell only a few feet wider than the previous one. This cell, however, was populated by another man in custody. He was a true vagrant, with a filthy beard and long hair matted to his scalp. He wore the same dirty clothes he'd been arrested in — long khaki pants and an oversized rain jacket that looked at least ten years old. He was reclined on a bench along one wall, facing the ceiling, fast asleep.

'The drunk tank,' D'Agostino said.

Slater didn't understand why he'd been moved, but he wasn't about to kick up a fuss. D'Agostino unlocked his cuffs and shoved him into the cell before he could do anything to retaliate. Slater stepped straight in through the gap in the steel bars, and D'Agostino yanked the door shut behind him. The homeless man remained fast asleep, knocked out by the alcohol in his system.

Why the hell did D'Agostino want him here? If Slater was in the commander's shoes, he would put the man he wanted dead in as isolated a place as he could manage. The other homeless guy was simply an additional potential witness.

Slater crossed to the other side of the windowless concrete box, breathing through his mouth because of his broken nose. Casting a glance across the floor of the holding cell, he realised he probably didn't want to be able to smell in any case. Dried vomit and other bodily fluids were caked across the concrete floor. Disgusted, Slater planted himself down on the opposite bench and set to work overcoming the pain of his shattered septum.

Still, D'Agostino lingered.

'I'll be back later,' he said.

Still, the homeless man didn't stir.

'I'm sure you will be,' Slater said.

'You're messing with the wrong guy.'

'You're the one killing vagrants. Which makes you the right guy.'

Bingo.

Slater had been preparing to drop the bombshell for some time, and by the way D'Agostino reacted he figured he'd nailed it. The police commander darted his gaze in every direction at once, searching for anyone who might have overheard the accusation. Finding nobody, he sent a dark look of fury in Slater's direction, then strode off down the corridor without a word.

Slater had made him angry.

He wondered what the night would entail.

The answer came only a couple of hours later.

Slater spent the time rolling with the waves of pain from his nose — the injury proved mind-numbingly annoying. Usually he was able to force all thoughts of his wounds in the field to the back of his mind until the task was complete, but in this instance the task entailed waiting around for hours in a dark concrete box with nothing but his own thoughts to keep him company. He could hardly focus on anything other than the pain in his head. But he fought time and time again to push the pain to a darker place, a place where he could retrieve it and deal with it later.

After a hundred and twenty minutes, Slater had most of the agony under control.

He'd elected to spread out across the bench and keep his eyes closed, pretending he was asleep until someone came for him. Whether that was normal cops or D'Agostino himself, he figured the best option regardless was to play up his vulnerability. So he stretched himself out, lying sideways on the cold steel, and kept one eye open a crack to observe what was happening in the corridor outside.

For hours, there was nothing.

The homeless guy across the cell must have consumed enough alcohol to kill a horse, because he didn't stir once in the time Slater spent reclined on the opposite bench. He snored and coughed and spluttered, but he didn't wake up.

Slater preferred that.

He didn't feel like striking up a conversation right now.

When D'Agostino returned, lumbering into Slater's vision with a switchblade in one hand and a steely expression on his face, Slater knew exactly why he'd been put in the drunk tank.

So there was someone to pin the following incident on.

The knife must have been retrieved from the evidence room, unless D'Agostino had left the station to purchase it. It was small enough to be feasibly concealed inside the homeless man's clothes, which would make an excellent cover story in the proceedings that followed. It was a simple enough explanation — two bums had started arguing and one had produced a weapon.

If there were no cameras capturing the proceedings, then it was D'Agostino's word against a homeless man who hadn't even been conscious at the time.

A foolproof cover story.

Slater didn't move a muscle. D'Agostino crept down the corridor, trying his best to keep quiet as he approached the cell, but Slater didn't react. He kept his eyes closed and his demeanour relaxed. He took a deep breath in, then released it over the course of a few seconds. It proved strangely difficult — acting calm and subdued in the face of a man coming to stab you to death.

But it was vital for what was to follow.

D'Agostino pulled to a halt in front of the cell and hovered behind the door for a long beat, his chest rising and falling, his gaze boring into Slater. Slater remained deathly still, seemingly passed out, completely vulnerable to attack.

Silently, D'Agostino unlocked the door.

He let the bars swing inward, and he stepped through into the cell, quiet as a mouse. He planted one boot on the dusty concrete floor and advanced forward.

Still, Slater didn't budge.

When D'Agostino came within a foot of the bench, Slater burst off it like a freight train, getting his feet underneath him before the bulky police commander could blink. D'Agostino jolted in place, suitably shocked by the sudden outburst, and made a wild thrust with the switchblade, stabbing forward in a kneejerk reaction. Slater saw it coming a mile away and twisted his body out of the way. The tip of the blade passed within a few inches of his spleen, then went sailing past.

And then Slater was in range.

And he was furious.

Game on.

He grabbed the back of D'Agostino's skull with one hand, and used the other arm to deliver an elbow that carried all the rage he'd been building for the past few hours. The point of his bone punched the commander's nose into the back of his head, completely destroying all the delicate tissue around the guy's septum, and shattering the nose itself.

A gruesome injury, all things considered, but Slater couldn't dredge up an ounce of remorse. Whatever this man was involved with in the dark heart of an unfinished skyscraper, it was worth protecting enough to kill any vagrants that stumbled across it.

That was reason enough to destroy the man's life.

The break caused such a sickening *crunch* to echo through the holding cell that for a moment Slater feared the homeless man might wake up. D'Agostino stumbled back, arms flailing, swinging wildly with the switchblade, hitting nothing but empty air. Slater grimaced as the knife came swinging past his throat from a wild haymaker.

Too close for comfort.

He drilled the ball of his foot into D'Agostino's gut, doubling the big man over as he tore a muscle in the guy's torso. Slater seized hold of the commander's head with both hands and smashed a knee into the side of his skull, targeting the soft skin above the ear.

Unconscious.

Like a switch being flipped.

All the energy sapped out of the man's limbs and he went down like a rag doll, sprawling across the floor of the cell with his nose broken and his hands empty. In one fluid motion Slater snatched the switchblade off the floor and planted it in the top of D'Agostino's skull, killing the man with a single downward swing. He wiped his hands on the man's jacket, stepped over his bloody corpse, and shut the door of the cell behind him as he left.

He guessed D'Agostino was a man of painstaking preparation, in which case all trace of Slater arriving at the station had been wiped from the archives of footage to provide the commander with an alibi. Unfortunately, due to extraneous circumstances, D'Agostino's whereabouts couldn't be accounted for, but who else could have murdered Slater other than the homeless man in the cell with him?

If the footage had been wiped as Slater suspected, then it would be a simple process of breaking out of the station and disappearing into the freezing Chicago night.

He could do that.

As he hurried down white brick corridors, keeping his face to the ground, he thought of what he'd done. He could've left the man unconscious in the cell, but he knew that he would soon be approaching the construction site to investigate, and what he found there would inevitably send him straight back to the station hunting for D'Agostino's head. It was easier to get the job done now.

Less messy.

Besides, all that moral trickery aside, D'Agostino had just tried to stab him to death.

That alone warranted an equal reaction on Slater's behalf.

So he barely gave it a second thought as he hurried away from the cell.

He reached the end of the corridor as it ran into a locked door that required authorised keycard access, and was halfway through positing how to overcome that particular obstacle when the door burst open in his face and a moronic Chicago P.D. officer came hurrying through.

11

T he guy hadn't even looked through the foggy glass partition to check whether there was anyone waiting on the other side of the door. He might as well have handed Slater his freedom on a silver platter.

Then again, not many people on this earth could take advantages of weaknesses the way Slater could.

The officer — a plain-looking Hispanic guy in his thirties — was already in the process of fumbling for the sidearm in its black leather holster at his waist when Slater put him down with a right hook to the jaw. He knew he would need to knock the man unconscious to avoid getting ambushed from behind minutes later, so he put as much force into the punch as he dared, annoyed that he had to incapacitate an innocent man but aware of the implications of leaving him alone.

The guy collapsed in a heap, shut off at the neurological light switch by the strike. He bounced off the opposite wall and came to rest slumped over in a seated position, chin drooped to his chest, well and truly unconscious. He would come around in less than a minute, but it would take him far longer than that to get his bearings and piece together what had happened.

By then, Slater figured he'd be miles away.

He relieved the officer of his Glock 17 and hurried straight through the open doorway, ignoring the tiny red light blinking on the display to indicate that a body had passed through the security checkpoint without scanning their keycard. He considered turning back and fishing the guard's pass out of his belt, but it simply wasn't worth the effort — ahead he saw the corridor open out into a wide lobby at the front of the station.

There would be a officer on the front desk for the night shift, without question.

Slater figured he could handle that.

As he hurried straight toward freedom it surprised him how drastically his life had changed in the space of a couple of years. Some time ago, he would have considered arrest a death sentence. Now, it was a simple inconvenience. His heart rate had barely elevated at the thought of being thrust into the holding cell, because he had the subliminal confidence to know he could manoeuvre his way out of nearly any situation.

Like the encounter that followed.

Without breaking stride he burst out into the open, maintaining a brisk pace through the lobby. He had the Glock trained on the man behind the reception desk before the guy realised what was happening. A pale man in his late twenties with thinning brown hair styled in a dreadful combover, he looked up from his papers after a beat of hesitation. Fear speared through his bleary eyes, and he froze on the spot.

The lobby was silent, save for Slater's thudding footsteps.

'Don't even think about moving,' Slater said. 'Stay right there and you'll be fine. Nod if you understand.'

The guy nodded, but there was nothing he could do regardless. By the time Slater had finished his sentence he'd already made it more than halfway across the tiled floor. Out of the corner of his eye Slater noticed the bulky shape of a surveillance camera positioned in the upper corner of the lobby, and he turned his face imperceptibly away from the line of sight.

The CCTV footage would pick up nothing but a dark-skinned man flying across the reception area in a blur.

He kept the barrel of the Glock trained rigidly on the desk grunt, unwavering in his intensity. Having memorised the route to the entrance doors, he didn't take his eyes off the guy. A cold sweat had broken out across the man's forehead, and he sported the expression of a deer in headlights. Slater had seen enough tense situations to know there was zero risk of the guy putting up a fight. The Glock's safety had been switched off by the mere act of resting his finger against the trigger, but he had no intention of actually firing his weapon. D'Agostino — as far as Slater knew — had been acting alone. If there were others, Slater would know soon enough.

The night was still young.

He shouldered the station door open and hurried out into the freezing darkness.

12

M ovement.

It was the only thing on Slater's mind.

He tucked the Glock out of sight as soon as he'd put a mile between himself and the station. Then he slid the same cheap smartphone out of the back pocket of his jeans — he couldn't believe that, in D'Agostino's haste to throw Slater in the drunk tank, the man hadn't had the mental fortitude to conduct a simple frisk search. Probably because of the stereotypes associated with vagrants. Besides, the man wouldn't have been thinking straight, internally panicking at the amount of knowledge Slater had about the construction site. Regular order and routine checks fell to the wayside when someone's life was in danger of being turned upside down.

Which turned Slater's attention to a vital point.

He had absolutely no idea what was happening inside the unfinished skyscraper.

He wasn't sure if he wanted to know. Whatever it was had warranted the murder of three homeless men found in the area, for the simple reason that they'd flown too close to the sun. D'Agostino had probably figured that, as commander for Chicago's central district, he had the authority and technical know-how to pass their deaths off as simple accidents.

Or set it up to look like a wild homeless brawl, in Slater's case.

And he'd paid for it with his life.

Slater hit dial on a number he'd memorised by heart and waited for the call to go through. Lars answered in seconds.

'What have you found?' the man said, understanding that Slater wouldn't be getting in touch unless he'd made progress.

'Ray D'Agostino.'

'What about him?'

'He's no longer with us.'

A pause.

A long pause.

'I won't lose my shit just yet,' Lars muttered, 'but how bad is it?'

'It's fine.'

'You know that if you're implicated, there's nothing we can do—'

'I said it's fine.'

'Where did it happen?'

'At the station.'

'Then it's very far from fine.'

'He came for me. Walked right into the holding cell with a switchblade. He was going to make it look like my cellmate stabbed me to death in a drunken brawl.'

Lars soaked that information in. 'So he would have switched off the cameras?'

'Exactly.'

The man breathed a sigh of relief. 'Okay. Is there anything that can pin you to the scene?'

'Maybe some murky CCTV footage from the exterior feeds. Nothing that'll be a problem, though.'

'We can probably make that disappear. I'll pull some strings.'

'How the hell are you going to do that?'

'Do we need to go over this again?' Lars said. 'You're the muscle. You don't get involved with the bureaucracy. Leave that to me. I'll take care of it.'

'Good.'

'Why'd he try to kill you?'

'It's the construction site. He's picking up vagrants from a specific area and slaughtering them if it sounds like they know anything about what's happening inside the skyscraper.'

'I don't know much about that place,' Lars said. 'I can start digging. I didn't think it would be the geographical area. I was thinking more along the lines of D'Agostino getting his kicks from killing people who couldn't fight back.'

'And it helps if no-one misses the victims.'

'Exactly.'

'It's not that. It's something bigger. I don't know what's going on, but it's worth killing over.'

An uncomfortable silence unfolded. 'And?'

Slater smirked, maintaining a vigorous pace through the darkened city. 'You think I'm getting cold feet?'

'I hope you're not.'

'Well, you'll be happy then. That's why I called.'

'For permission?'

'To sniff around.'

'You should know by now that you don't need permission.'

'Oh?'

'Slater,' Lars said, his voice stern. 'You just killed a police commander in his own station and I didn't bat an eyelid. You think I'll have a problem with you investigating further?'

'So no matter what happens,' Slater said, 'there won't be repercussions?'

'Within reason. If it comes out that you've slaughtered innocent civilians we'll need to take measures to prevent you from doing any further damage.'

'I'd never do anything like that.'

'We know. That's why we recruited you.'

Slater had made it almost a mile away from the central district precinct when the echo of a distant police siren trickled down the open street. He threw a glance over his shoulder, suddenly paranoid. D'Agostino had been one corrupt bastard, but that didn't change the circumstances. Slater had murdered an officer of the law in one of the most brutal fashions imaginable, and any kind of arrest would result in Black Force denying his existence. He would be left to rot in a prison cell for the rest of his life, or receive the death sentence for his endeavours. There would be no way to connect D'Agostino to a yet-unknown plot within an abandoned construction site, and Slater couldn't see a path to successfully defending himself if he was apprehended.

So he ducked into the lee of a neighbouring alleyway, allowing the darkness to envelop him. He paused there for a long ten count with the smartphone pressed to his ear, eyes darting left and right in search of confrontation. At this point he wouldn't shy away from barrelling straight through an army of police officers if it resulted in his own freedom.

But nothing materialised.

No-one came.

The street remained dark and silent and empty. The street lights spaced intermittently along the two-lane road did little to penetrate the night. In the alleyway itself, Slater could barely see his hand in front of his face.

On the other end of the line, Lars sensed that Slater had gone quiet. He didn't respond, remaining silent until Slater opted to voice his concerns.

After a long beat, Slater muttered, 'All clear.'

'You being hunted?'

'I can't imagine D'Agostino's body will go undiscovered for long.'

'Anyone else get a good look at you on the way out of the station?'

'One guy saw me for a couple of seconds but he won't remember anything.'

'Knocked him out?'

'Yeah.'

'You're particularly good at that.'

'That's something you've observed?'

'You just seem to have a knack for it.'

'It's not hard when you get the hang of it.'

'I wouldn't know. I'm a desk jockey.'

Slater smirked. 'So just to clarify — I'm all clear to check out this construction site?'

'I don't think you understand the concept of the division you work for. You can do whatever the hell you want. You don't exist.'

Slater twisted on the spot to glance down the alleyway, suddenly spooked. Finding nothing, he hunched over the phone. 'I think I'm slowly coming to that realisation.'

'Go knock some heads together.'

'Happily,' Slater said.

He ended the call and tucked the phone back into his pocket. Exhilarated by the sheer thrill of the operation, he strode straight back out onto the sidewalk and surged with purpose in the same direction he'd been heading.

Into the unknown.

13

S later had only undertaken three missions for Black Force, but they had taught him more about the workings of the world than anything he'd experienced previously.

There were certain social cues and standard interactions that, if exploited successfully, resulted in phenomenal success in the field. Slater had been experimenting with a wide range of techniques over the last six months, and over time it had started to open his mind to the power of a proper approach.

Like right now.

He spotted the construction site in the distance, as dormant as when he'd first laid eyes on it. Its half-finished structure twisted into the night sky, dwarfed by the gleaming skyscrapers on either side but set far enough back from the street to go largely unnoticed unless you paid attention to it. The sidewalk in front of the site lay desolate, unpopulated.

There wasn't a soul in sight.

Slater figured he would have spooked D'Agostino with

all his talk, especially if the police commander imagined
that Slater knew the truth about his business inside the site.
Slater put himself in the man's shoes, and figured he would
have put his operation — whatever that may be — on lock-
down until Slater was dead and D'Agostino could check the
coast was clear and nothing was amiss.

Which would involve a trip to the construction site.

Which meant whoever dwelled within the structure
would be expecting D'Agostino.

So Slater kept his shoulders straight and his chest out,
refusing to allow any shred of hesitation to creep into his
demeanour. It would be paramount in the coming
moments. As he crossed the street he stared up at the
gargantuan structure with all its dark walkways and
crevices, and figured he was definitely being watched. He
nodded up at the giant construction site, holding up three
fingers in an arbitrary gesture. It meant nothing, but it made
him look like he was in the loop.

And sometimes, in the world of crime and espionage,
that was all it took to carve out an opening.

An opening was all a man of Slater's calibre needed.

He stepped up onto the sidewalk in front of the
skyscraper and strode straight into the site, squeezing
through a narrow gap in the rusting wire fence. Gravel
crunched underfoot, signalling his presence, but Slater had
already made clear the fact that he wasn't hiding. He made
as much noise as he wanted as he ducked under low-
hanging scaffolding and powered further away from the
street lights until the darkness swamped him. He didn't dare
use his phone as a flashlight — he wasn't sure what would
be taken as a threat and what wouldn't.

He continued straight into the bowels of the construction site, keeping the Glock in the back of his jeans,

unwilling to cause confrontation just yet. He was vulnerable to a surprise attack — if the people populating the skyscraper wanted him dead on the spot, they could simply shoot him in the back. They no doubt knew the layout of the site far better than he did.

It was one of the more foolish moves in military history, no doubt — Slater couldn't imagine a soldier displaying such insane foolhardiness to stride unprepared into enemy territory. But Slater's work took place in the strange, muddied grey area of society — no-one knew he was a government operative. He could use susceptibility to his advantage, and he did so now.

When the twin flashlights lit up the corridor around him, spearing through the darkness and illuminating him where he stood, he didn't flinch.

When the twin beams lowered to the floor, casting shadows across the walls and revealing a pair of muscular Eastern European men standing a dozen feet ahead, scrutinising him, he acted like there was nothing out of the ordinary.

When he noticed the flashlight attached to automatic rifles, he didn't bat an eyelid.

He simply stood in place and pretended like he belonged.

He found that particular gesture worked an uncanny amount of times.

And when the barrels of the rifles remained trained on the floor, Slater realised he had the window of opportunity he'd been so desperately searching for.

Simultaneously, it confirmed D'Agostino's involvement in something menacing.

A weight lifted off his shoulders. On the trek from the police station to the construction site, doubts had plagued him intermittently, trying to convince him that he'd made an error and killed an innocent man. But, time and time again, he turned back to the image of Ray D'Agostino descending on the cell with a murderous glint in his eyes and a switchblade in his hand.

That immediately dispelled any thoughts of making a mistake.

Even if there was nothing at the construction site, Slater felt nothing for killing a man who had tried to take his own life.

That was the risk one took when dealing with a trained specialist.

The two Eastern European men advanced, their physiques akin to muscle-packed gorillas. They were both big and burly and their tight jackets strained against their massive arms. Slater figured he would lose an arm wrestle to them.

But he wouldn't lose a fight.

14

Slater nodded to each of them in turn — they didn't respond with any kind of acknowledgement, but they didn't aim their weapons at him either, and that was all he asked for. He stayed on the spot to minimise his own aggression, allowing them to approach instead. If he had to guess, he would have picked them as Dagestanis, but it was hard to discern the difference between the specific regions of Eastern Europe.

Whatever the case, they were hard, cruel men.

Slater could see it in their eyes.

'Who the fuck are you?' one of them demanded, his accent thick.

They were the first words spoken since the two parties had laid eyes on each other. The five syllables echoed off the walls, highlighting the isolation of the construction site. They were deep inside the skyscraper now, in unfinished halls, within the vicinity of no-one.

Lots of room to bury a body in here.

There was hostility in the man's tone, and in both their demeanours — that was inevitable. But it wasn't the kind of unwavering aggression that would result in Slater catching a bullet if he made the wrong move. Instead it was the kind of typical anger and frustration that came with having to deal with an unknown party.

They thought he was involved with D'Agostino in some capacity. They simply didn't know how to react to him.

There was a vast difference between that, and wanting to shoot him dead where he stood.

Because who the hell would stride willingly into this darkened structure if they didn't have business within?

'Ray sent me,' Slater muttered, sending a piercing glare at both men to try and assert dominance.

At the mention of the police commander, both men twitched. The man on the left — the one who had spoken first — shifted uncomfortably on the spot. 'He did not mention this.'

'Were you expecting him in the flesh?'

'*Da.*'

'Yeah, well,' Slater said, then cast a glance over his shoulder to sell the performance. 'There's been unexpected developments.'

'Huh?'

Slater beckoned with two fingers, urging the first man forward, as confident as always in his intentions. Sensing Slater's brashness, the first guy shuffled a couple of steps further toward him. Now they were only half a foot apart.

Dangerously close.

Not that the man knew it.

'Someone at the station,' Slater mumbled, deliberately quietening his voice. 'They figured out what was happening here.'

'Police?'

Slater nodded.

'So who are you?' the first man said, but there was far less hostility in his tone this time. There was genuine concern, unease that law enforcement might be descending on the structure at any moment.

It was the oldest trick in the book. Slater had subliminally aligned his intentions with the men — even though he had no proof that he was who he said he was, they trusted him because of the mutual threat of being caught. They were united in their involvement in the operation, even though Slater wasn't involved at all.

But they didn't know that.

'I'm the muscle,' Slater said. 'Ray sent me to take care of things.'

'What things?'

'The guy at the station, for starters. The one who realised what was happening.'

'This station man,' the first guy said in broken English. 'Who?'

Slater inclined his head toward the floor, hunching forward as if he had secrets to share. The first Dagestani took another imperceptible step in Slater's direction. Now their heads were separated by mere inches, as if Slater was about to whisper a revelation in the man's ear.

And he did.

'Me.'

15

It threw the guy off for a second — he hadn't been expecting Slater to admit that kind of information. He paused for the briefest of moments in time as the gears whirred in his head, connecting the dots and understanding the fact that the stranger in front of him had sinister intentions.

By that point it was already too late.

Slater activated all his fast-twitch muscle fibres at once, transitioning from a state of calm to an explosive battering ram that threw everything with murderous intent. He launched a thunderous right hook that scythed through the shadows and connected with every knuckle at once on the side of the Dagestani's head, drilling into the soft skin right above the man's left ear.

Lars' words proved correct.

Slater did have a knack for smashing people unconscious.

The guy dropped with no control of his limbs, folding over like a lawn chair and crumpling into the loose dirt underfoot. The floor of the hallways on the ground level hadn't been installed yet, and the dirt softened the impact as the first guy went down. As a result, his comrade didn't notice the sudden explosive shift in atmosphere until his chance of retaliation had dissipated.

Slater leapt over the first guy's prone form and transferred all his forward momentum into a jumping front kick that concluded with the heel of his boot crushing into the second guy's sternum. Hurt but not unconscious, the second guy uttered an uncontrollable grunt of surprise and spiralled into the far wall, the breath stripped from his lungs and the assault rifle stripped from his hands.

With both guns now on the floor, the light vanished. A thin glow of luminescence filtered along the dirt, but everything more than a few inches above the ground remained shrouded in darkness. Slater could barely make out the silhouette of the second guy bouncing off the half-finished plaster wall, stumbling for balance in the narrow corridor.

But one glimpse was all he needed.

He surged forward and let fly with three consecutive punches to the guy's exposed torso, using his left fist, then his right, then returning to the left. It only took a little over a second to deliver the three blows, and they sapped what little energy the man had right out of him. He doubled over, and Slater sensed his opportunity.

Slater dropped the point of his elbow into the back of the man's head, flattening him into the dirt and transporting him to the same realm as his unconscious buddy a few feet away.

The corridor became still again.

Slater's brain went haywire, immediately assessing the aftermath of the conflict.

By this point he'd been in enough life or death fights to understand the emotions racing through him. Sure, he was technically an elite black operations warrior, but the chemical cocktail that floods your brain in the aftermath of shocking violence can't be avoided.

Slater rested one hand against the half-finished wall of the corridor and took a couple of deep breaths in and out, settling his racing heart. The burst of adrenalin racing through his mind, supercharging his limbs with unnatural intensity, threatened to overwhelm him. He had grappled with it before, but it always took sizeable effort to control.

And those who could control it won the war.

His instincts told him to charge straight through the construction site and beat down anyone he laid eyes on. It was his body's natural response to the fight. There were all manner of ways to try and deny the fact that beating adversaries into the dirt wasn't intoxicating, but Slater had long ago stopped pretending to ignore it.

If you can embrace that fact, you can work on taming it.

In truth, it felt damn good to destroy competition so effortlessly. Slater had spent years of his life toiling away without a day off, slaving his mind and body to their physical limits in MMA gyms and, more recently, state-of-the-art training facilities created by Lars Crawford to develop elite soldiers. He was at the pinnacle of athletic achievement, which made it fairly effortless to gain the upper hand on thugs like the two men at his feet.

And remaining clinical and measured in the face of such power often proved difficult.

But Slater was getting the hang of it.

Even though his brain screamed at him to throw caution to the wind and take off into the bowels of the skyscraper, trying to convince himself that he could overcome any adversity he faced, he allowed the silence to settle back over the hallway. The two flashlights on the ground maintained their thin sheen of illumination — Slater stared at them for a moment, then paced over to the bulky torches and stamped down on each of them. Glass shattered and the lights flickered out, plunging the corridor back into total darkness. It would be foolish to heft one of the enormous devices into one hand and stroll aimlessly through the structure, signalling his presence in the most obvious way possible.

Instead he embraced the blackness and silently retrieved the two automatic rifles from their last known locations on the floor — they were Kalashnikovs of some kind, a staple on the black market, but Slater didn't have time to fumble around in the darkness and discern their exact model. He deposited the two cumbersome weapons in a gap between the plaster boards, tucking them out of sight in case the two thugs woke up. Then he slid the Glock 17 out of his waistband, automatically disengaging the trigger safety by resting his index finger against it.

There was no need to employ trigger discipline in this hostile environment.

He had seen enough action to employ restraint if he spotted an innocent person. He wouldn't impulsively fire on anything that moved. But at the same time, he wanted to be ready to retaliate to any violence at the drop of a hat.

His cover had been blown.

He didn't need to blend in anymore. He hoped there wasn't an army of Eastern European gangsters in this construction site. He hadn't come here for a war.

He had come here for answers.

Then a noise burst through the absolute quiet. Slater picked up the soft sound on the edge of his hearing, and he nearly jolted in surprise. He hadn't been expecting anything like what he'd just heard.

The pitiful whimper of a child.

16

I t had come from the ground floor, filtering through the darkness in the kind of eerie manner ordinarily reserved for horror movies. At any moment Slater expected to follow the sound to its bloody conclusion, but instead of being ambushed by a demonic presence he would find himself embroiled in a vicious war with a party of Eastern European thugs.

What did you get yourself wrapped up in, D'Agostino? he thought.

But there was no time to dwell on what could be. Possibilities meant nothing in his field. He needed concrete information, data to see and process and react to.

So he didn't think twice about heading straight into the unknown.

Even though it might result in his life being cut awfully short.

He hurried further into the construction site, keeping as quiet as he was able, leaving the pair of gangsters behind. They would soon regain consciousness — this wasn't the movies, and people recovered from being stripped of their senses in seconds — but they would find themselves in complete darkness, free of their weapons, clawing their way around and trying to determine what the hell had happened.

Slater didn't pay them a second thought — they might shout for help, but that would work in his favour. He embraced confusion and hysteria. He was one man against an unknown number of hostiles, and anything that turned the tide of panic against his adversaries he would happily accept.

He took his tentative time ghosting down the corridor. Another whimper floated through the darkness, but this time it was harshly cut off mid-cry. The noise itself was barely perceptible, but the rest of the sob had been muffled, as if someone had clamped a hand over the child's mouth.

Slater's guts twisted into a knot. He never liked involving innocents. He would have given anything to be isolated in this construction site with gangsters and mercenaries and street thugs, free to dish out punishment as he saw fit. Bringing someone who didn't deserve to die into the equation only ever resulted in disaster.

But that was how the situation was unfolding, and that was what he would have to deal with.

It was his job to improvise and find solutions.

He strained his eyes for any sign of the path ahead — worst case scenario, he would use his phone's flashlight, which was far less noticeable than one of the thug's enormous torches. But he glimpsed the faintest outline of a darker space in the left-hand side of the wall ahead. The tiniest shred of illumination from the streetlights far behind him was trickling through the minuscule gaps in the construction site's exterior, allowing him to barely see the way ahead and make sure he wasn't about to stumble over an enormous drop.

He saw the doorway.

He shifted the Glock into a ready position, and crept straight through into the dark space within. He kept his centre of mass low, hunching over and bending at the knees to minimise the target area any potential hostiles had to work with. He froze only a foot inside the doorway, not making a sound, the couple of footfalls he'd taken to step inside the room producing no noise whatsoever. If there were people a few feet in front of him, they wouldn't have heard him.

But at the same time, he couldn't see them either.

Patience was steadily becoming Slater's specialty. Even though he'd utilised maximum effort to beat two men into the ground only thirty seconds earlier, now he poised still as a statue inside the doorway, listening for the slightest hint of human presence.

He found it in seconds.

'What do we do?' the child's voice breathed, only a couple of feet from Slater's position. The kid had uttered the words in a tone below a whisper, barely vocalising any noise whatsoever.

But Slater heard it.

He remained deathly still.

The kid had been searching for guidance, expecting answers to his enquiries, wanting someone in a position of authority to lead the way.

There was someone else here.

In this room.

Right next to him.

'Shh,' another voice breathed in response — this one older, throatier, female.

A woman.

The mother?

Slater didn't budge an inch.

'Quiet,' the woman continued, maintaining the same decibel level as the kid, her words almost unnoticeable, even in the absolute silence. 'I think there's someone close by.'

Slater couldn't stay put any longer. The general atmosphere around him indicated that there were no hostiles. He didn't think there was another gang of Eastern European thugs in this room — they wouldn't be able to maintain this kind of silence. Even if they had guns pressed to the child and woman's heads, they would make noticeable adjustments. They would shift around, or quietly demand the hostages to shut their fucking mouths.

Slater reached back, moving an inch at a time, and slid the smartphone out of his back pocket.

He activated the flashlight with the soft tap of a finger.

Harsh white light speared through the small room and the woman — sitting with her back against the wall right near the doorway — stifled a scream of surprise. To make sure she didn't follow through with the piercing noise, Slater swung the barrel of the Glock around in a tight arc and jammed it against her forehead, pressing the back of her skull against the wall with just enough force to let her know he meant business.

In the newly formed light, he bore an icy stare directly into her eyes, silently instructing her to stay completely quiet.

She obeyed.

Slater processed what he could see.

The woman was in her early thirties with high cheekbones and a porcelain-like quality to her skin — probably a mixture of fright and a naturally pale complexion. She was undeniably beautiful, with an athletic frame and long blonde hair pulled back tight in a ponytail. She wore a full body tracksuit and dirty sneakers, and her left wrist hung uselessly a couple of feet off the ground, chained to the wall by a single handcuff and a bolt.

Alongside her were two kids.

They were both young — Slater estimated between four and six — and were in similar predicaments, one of their limbs each chained to the wall. The three sat only half a foot apart, lined up just inside the doorway. The rest of the room was threadbare, half-finished before construction on the skyscraper had seemingly shut down, all the developments that had been made on the ground floor already falling into disrepair.

Slater saw all he needed, and turned the light back off instantly.

'Don't panic,' he said under his breath, sporting the same volume as the previous exchanges. 'I'm here to get you out.'

17

The darkness seemed to terrify the woman, who Slater deemed the only one of the three capable of conversing with him. He wasn't about to interrogate a pair of kids — they had enough problems already. Beyond the barrel of his Glock he sensed her shaking, and the atmosphere in the room seemed to turn colder than usual.

'I'm not going to hurt you,' Slater whispered.

'The gun,' she said, barely able to spit the two syllables out, her voice weak.

'If I take it away, do you promise not to scream?'

'Of course. I'm not stupid.'

'I know you're not. But this is an incredibly stressful situation. People do crazy—'

'Take the fucking gun off my head!' she hissed under her breath.

Slater nodded in the darkness, a useless gesture, and lowered the Glock. So far there was no sign of life anywhere else on the ground floor. He hoped the two thugs he'd dealt with a minute earlier were the only kind of resistance he'd face for the foreseeable future.

'Who are you?' she said, remarkably composed.

'Just a guy who wants to help.'

'Bullshit. I heard all that nonsense out in the corridor. You're involved somehow. Who's D'Agostino? Why am I here?'

Slater paused, allowing the woman to spill all her thoughts before responding. 'Did you hear a few muffled thumps?'

'Yeah. What was—?'

'Those two guys aren't much of a problem anymore. Trust me now?'

'No.'

'Well, right now I'm the only person capable of getting you out of those cuffs. So I'd trust me if I were you.'

Slater was about to ask for anything he could use to piece together what was happening in the construction site, and why a woman and two children were chained to a wall on the ground floor, but before he could get another sentence out she threw him off with a single question.

'Where's the rest of the guys on this floor?'

'What?'

'What did you do with them?'

'Nothing.'

'Oh.'

She went quiet, simultaneously coming to the same realisation as Slater. As if on cue thudding footsteps exploded into earshot, materialising at the foot of the corridor he'd just come from. Someone cursed viciously in Russian, and there was the sound of a semi-conscious body being hefted off the floor.

Not good.

'Who the fuck did this?' a Russian voice snapped.

'Down there,' one of the men Slater had attacked said, his voice drowsy, barely able to hold it together.

He must have signalled in the correct direction, because a second later Slater sensed three or four pairs of boots crunching through the loose dirt toward his location. In the darkness the sound amplified, horrifying close, approaching fast. They must have known exactly where the hostages were being kept and made a beeline for the doorway.

He barely had time to get his feet underneath him. Slater prided himself on a frighteningly quick reaction speed, but even that didn't help him here. The rapidity with which the hostile bodies poured into the room caught him entirely off-guard, and it took his brain a moment to flip the switch back into primal survival mode.

But when he entered that state, there was no stopping him.

His thoughts were consumed by the fact that there were two children in the room. It supercharged him with the kind of vigour he couldn't tap into often — the sheer, unbridled intensity that came from the knowledge that a pair of kids and what seemed to be their mother would die painfully if he didn't succeed.

So when the first man to enter the room ran straight into Slater in the darkness, fumbling with the under-barrel flashlight on his weapon, Slater showed zero restraint.

He wrapped the back of the guy's head in a Muay Thai clinch, clasping one hand around the man's skull, and fired off two consecutive knees into the bridge of the man's nose. There was a weapon somewhere between them — Slater felt the uncomfortable jab of a bulky assault rifle against his stomach — but the barrel wasn't pointed in his direction. Everything had unfolded too fast. Slater shattered bones in the guy's face before he could get a shot off, and the man crumpled.

Either from the sheer pain of his injuries, or because he'd been stripped of consciousness.

One down.

Slater hurled his unresisting body to the side and spotted two more silhouettes appearing instantly in the doorway. Even in the total darkness he spotted the unmistakable outline of automatic weapons, and he didn't hesitate. He raised the Glock 17 and fired twice at the man on the left. The muzzle flares lit up the room for a half-second, and as the first man crumpled Slater used the brief burst of light to lock up his aim with the guy on the right.

It only took one more shot.

Three down.

Barely able to put a cohesive thought together because of the jolt of energy to his bones, Slater took off in a running start and hurled himself through the open doorway, anticipating a fourth combatant to come tearing into sight at any moment.

Not that he could see anything in the carnage, anyway.

But instead of diving over the threshold and hitting the dirt a second later, he thundered into a body halfway through his spear tackle, meeting some kind of centre mass that sent both parties sprawling to the dirt in a tangle of limbs. Slater bounced off the ground, nerve endings firing across his shoulders and back — he considered himself lucky not to have broken his neck in the reckless assault.

But it had thrown both of them off-guard, and if there was one thing Slater had confidence in, it was his ability to capitalise on an even playing field.

Which was exactly what he'd been intending in the first place.

He maintained momentum as soon as he hit the ground and rolled closer to the last remaining hostile, coming down awkwardly on top of the man in the wide open hallway. The guy's Kalashnikov became pinned between them, sandwiched between their respective weights.

The guy underneath him struggled, cursing in Russian, spraying Slater with spit.

He didn't care.

He'd somehow lost the Glock in the chaos, but he simply got his feet underneath him and wrestled the Kalashnikov off the guy with brute force. Instead of spending the valuable time fumbling over the weapon in the blackness, checking whether the safety was off and the reliable rifle was ready to fire, Slater simply treated the gun as a bat and brought it down with a *thwack* against the guy's skull.

Once again — silence.

Slater walked straight back into the room with the hostages, subconsciously glad that the conflict had taken place in the dark.

He didn't really want to see the results of his rifle swing. From the sound of the impact, the thug was dead. That was all he needed to know.

Ears ringing from the unsuppressed gunshots, painfully aware of the racket that had been caused, Slater grimaced.

The situation had become a ticking time bomb.

18

He could barely hear a thing after the three shots he'd fired.

The room containing the three hostages had no windows or gaps in the walls aside from the doorway itself. As a result the sound of the gunshots had been contained, amplified by the confined space, to such an extent that the high-pitched whining in Slater's ears caused him genuine pain. Convinced he'd given himself long-term hearing issues, he crouched low in the centre of the room, maintaining a calm demeanour in the face of total carnage.

'It's me,' he said to the dark room, his words sounding hollow with his impaired hearing.

He wasn't sure if the woman or the kids could hear him, but he didn't want them panicking — he wanted them to know they were temporarily safe. He couldn't risk turning on a flashlight, but it seemed foolish to try and calm them down.

He had just incapacitated four people in front of their eyes.

Nothing happened for a long time. A minute passed,

and Slater remained still as a statue, eyes fixed on the dark gap in the wall where the doorway rested, waiting for reinforcements to come charging in.

Ready to deal with any further threats.

Finding none, he started to grow optimistic. Maybe it was a six-man setup. Maybe he'd killed everyone in the construction site who posed a threat. Maybe D'Agostino's operation was done.

But nothing ever went according to plan.

When some semblance of his hearing began to return, he deemed it prudent to continue the conversation with the woman, even though he wasn't sure how mentally scarred she would be from the proceedings.

'What's your name?' he said quietly, trying to inject some shred of normality into the situation.

'Theresa,' she said.

'Theresa, I'm Will.'

'You killed those men?'

'Yes.'

Neither of the kids piped up — Slater imagined they were both in a state of shock. Theresa, on the other hand, seemed surprisingly calm.

'You okay?' he said.

'Fine.'

'You sure?'

'Just get me out of here, okay?'

'These guys kidnapped you?'

She nodded. 'And my children.'

'You three are a family?'

'Yes.'

'When did it happen?'

'Earlier today.'

'Time?'

'Roughly four p.m.'

'How'd it happen?'

'We were shopping. There's a detour we usually take. Through an alley. They got us there.'

'Shoved you into a van?'

'Pretty much. It happened really fast.'

'You're married?'

'Yes.'

'And he's the father of these kids?'

'Yes.'

'How do you think he'll react to this?'

'He'll be devastated.'

'He'd do anything to get you back?'

'Yes.'

'Even pay an enormous ransom?'

'Yes.'

'You have money?'

'Yes.'

'What do you do?'

'He's a lawyer. I run an online business. Jewellery.'

'Big shot lawyer?'

'I guess.'

'Does he seem like the type of guy to play along with any demands?'

'What do you mean?'

Slater pressed a pair of fingers into his closed eyelids, battling down an oncoming headache, connecting the dots between this particular incident and a story told to him by a model named Florence earlier that evening.

'Just seems like there's a pattern here in Chicago,' he muttered. 'And I have a feeling your husband's being deliberately targeted.'

'I don't understand...' Theresa whispered.

'What type of lawyer is he?'

'Criminal defence.'

'He co-operates with the Chicago P.D. occasionally?'

'Of course. Part of the job.'

'You think he has friends in the force?'

'I know he does. Actually, that name you mentioned earlier. Out in the corridor...'

'D'Agostino?'

'Yes. Stephen's met with him a few times. You think...?'

'I know,' Slater said.

It would be easy, wouldn't it?

As a police commander, you would make acquaintances with wealthy types — mostly lawyers, especially in the field of law enforcement. You would come to learn which of them were vulnerable to exploitation, and from there it would be fairly straightforward. Recruit a small force of hired goons looking for work in the Chicago underworld — maybe even use your experience running the central district to find the easiest nodes through which you could hire mercenaries. Abduct the wealthy target's family, but use your vast experience as an officer of the law to do it in the most efficient way possible. Leave no trace of what you've done. Demand ransom, leaning on all kinds of pressure points that you discovered whilst befriending the husbands. When the money's received, return the families safe and sound and insist that if a word is uttered about this incident, there will be blood to spill. Keep your identity disguised and anonymous the entire time. Let the Dagestanis handle the grunt work. After a few days pass and no-one goes forward to the police, too scared to act, the entire thing will be swept under the rug, never to be discussed or referred to again.

Because the best crimes made the victims implicit.

Because that's what true master manipulators, like Commander Ray D'Agostino, were able to do.

But what about when the husbands didn't co-operate?

Slater didn't want to know how long D'Agostino had been running this operation. It would no doubt come to light, when news of his death hit the newspapers and television, and his dark empire slowly emerged from the shadows. Witnesses would come forward. They wouldn't have known it was D'Agostino at the time, but they would connect the dots. The pieces would fall into place.

A hostage operation carried out with the painstaking detail of a commander who knew exactly how to get away with any kind of crime.

Genius.

But Slater had no time to consider D'Agostino's empire, because Theresa piped up. 'Will?'

Her voice was shaking.

'What?' Slater said.

'Are you sure you killed those men?'

'What are you talking about?'

'It's just... I heard something.'

The first guy.

Slater's heart rate skyrocketed and he yanked the phone out of his back pocket, not interested in keeping quiet anymore. He turned the flashlight on, revealing something worse than the first guy regaining consciousness.

The man simply wasn't there anymore.

19

S later recalled the damage his strikes would have caused. Two undefended knees directly to the nose — the man's septum would have shattered and it probably would have briefly knocked him unconscious.

But he must have recovered just enough to get his feet under him and slip unobstructed out of the room, taking advantage of the darkness and Slater's distracted state. He'd been processing everything Florence had told him, grappling with the coincidence that her story was connected with D'Agostino and the operation in the skyscraper. Now he found himself reeling — he'd lost a hostile, one that knew where he was and what he was armed with.

He couldn't let the guy escape.

But it looked like the man already had.

Slater wheeled on the spot, bringing the flashlight over to illuminate the three hostages. He got a look at the two kids for the first time — both were ghostly white, shaking and shivering and staring up at him with wide eyes and dilated pupils. He wasn't sure whether they'd been drugged or not, but they were scared out of their minds.

He didn't blame them.

Inwardly, he was too.

Racing through a laundry list of ways to respond to the crisis, he turned to face Theresa. Despite her relatively calm answers to Slater's questions, she seemed in a similar state to her kids.

'Theresa,' he said, ignoring the horrified expression on her face as she glimpsed the three dead bodies lying across the threshold to the room, only a few feet away from her. He imagined the family didn't have much experience with blood and violence.

Sometimes he wished he didn't either.

But he was slowly beginning to accept the fact that this situation felt perfectly normal.

He was steadily becoming accustomed to the over-whelming wave of emotions that plagued every life or death encounter.

He was learning to get comfortable being uncomfortable.

And he hasn't lost all control of the situation.

Yet.

'Theresa,' he repeated, and finally she took her eyes away from the bodies.

'Yes?'

'What else can you tell me? Are there more?'

'More what?'

'More thugs. The guys who kidnapped you.'

She looked at him as if he were stupid. 'Of course there's more.'

Slater sensed the blood draining from his cheeks. He battled down a racing heart and wiped his sweaty palms against his jeans. 'Okay. How many more?'

'At least ten. This place is crawling with them.'

'Ten?!'

'Well, you've killed a few. Maybe six or seven left. It's an entire convoy of those Russian guys. They all look the same. They're all horrible.'

'I can't hear anyone approaching. And I fired my weapon two minutes ago. What does—?'

Theresa audibly gasped. 'Oh, God. Will. Move!'

'What?'

'They'll be dealing with the collateral. Oh, no. Oh my God. Go!'

He seized her by the shoulder. 'What the hell are you on about?'

'There's more families. Upstairs.'

'Fuck. Why are you down here, then?'

'We're new arrivals. I guess this is like a... holding cell.'

'How far upstairs?'

'We got taken up there. Right at the start. I think seven or eight floors up. They have it all set up flawlessly. I saw three different families. Women and children. So six total. I'm the only person kidnapped with two kids. It's probably logistically harder.'

'You're good at feeding me information,' Slater noted.

'My husband's a lawyer. Will, you need to—'

Slater got to his feet and stared at one of the discarded Kalashnikovs in the doorway — an AK-15, he noted, now that he was illuminating the room with the phone flashlight. It struck him as odd that the Eastern European thug who had fled the room moments earlier hadn't picked up one of the assault rifles and drilled a cluster of rounds through the back of Slater's head whilst he'd been distracted.

But the room would have been pitch dark, and Slater had already punched the guy's nose into the back of his skull, so he certainly hadn't been thinking straight. He would have got to his feet and hurried straight out of the room, as quiet as he could.

To raise the alarm.

Slater realised he needed to move, just as Theresa had demanded. When the thug reached the top floor and informed his friends that the three gunshots they'd heard earlier hadn't been their imagination and that there really was a trained hostile inside the building, all the other families being kept in the skyscraper would be placed in danger.

Who knew what a pack of unhinged guns-for-hire would do when their operation was in jeopardy?

Slater didn't want to find out.

He needed to get the jump on them before they could do anything brash.

Already drained from the energy he'd exerted so far, he clambered to his feet and tightened his grip on both the Glock 17 and the smartphone's flashlight.

Taking a deep breath, he muttered, 'Be right back,' and plunged straight into the unknown.

20

E xpecting confrontation right off the bat, he found himself somewhat surprised to find the ground floor devoid of life. He raced through unfinished hallways and ducked under dirty steel beams, largely unsure of where he was headed, left with almost no information about what he would be running into.

He'd never been this unprepared in his life.

He'd elected to leave the Kalashnikovs behind — in such close quarters he preferred the ease with which he could wield a Glock. Not that it mattered, anyway. He spent the entire duration of the sprint strangely certain of his own impending death. The icy terror settling over him did nothing to calm his heart rate — his operations for Black Force had been pulse-pounding to date, but nothing like this.

He was heading up the stairwell of a half-finished skyscraper in the freezing cold, armed with a pistol, tasked with eliminating a small army of Eastern European thugs who had three innocent families to use as hostages and human shields.

Teeth chattering — he told himself it was the cold — he reached the barren stairwell after only twenty seconds of racing through the building's ground floor. He stared up at the gaping maw above, unnerved by the scale of the spiralling vertical tunnel. It consisted of a giant rectangular space spearing up toward the night sky far above, running through largely unfinished levels of the skyscraper's bottom half. The open air provided a little more natural light to work with — everything was shrouded in a dark blue hue instead of consumed by complete darkness. There was nothing to shield a fall through the central tunnel of the stairwell — no barricades, no walls. Just an eight-storey cylinder of open space riddled with the occasional stretch of scaffolding.

Slater hurried straight up the concrete stairs without a second thought.

There was no sign of activity. He doubted the Eastern Europeans would have sentries manning the access points — they didn't seem like they had that level of intelligence. They would be in panic mode, debating what to do about the unsuppressed gunshots from below just as their comrade came racing into sight with his face caved in and blood pouring out of his nose, warning about a single intruder tearing through their forces.

They might not believe him.

Good.

Slater would take all the hesitation he could get.

The desolation of the construction site leeched through the atmosphere — Slater figured the three gunshots would have simply sounded like a car backfiring from out on the street. The structure was gargantuan, no doubt intended to act as the home for a giant corporate firm upon completion. But evidently the builders had gone into liquidation, or the

developers had run out of money, or any number of problems had cropped up that were common in the corporate
world.

As he raced up the stairs with the cool night air on his
face and the barren concrete walls dwarfing him on all
sides, Slater began to connect the dots.

D'Agostino's connections with the city council might
have notified him about this place. He could have subtly
swept the building's documents under the rug, pretending
to pass them along the supply chain but in fact hiding all
knowledge of the abandoned construction site's existence.
Then he would be free to use it as he pleased, not having to
worry about the council seizing the land.

Sometimes it paid to hold a position of authority.

You could get away with murder.

If Slater thought his heart was racing earlier, he wasn't
prepared for the fatigue that set in as he reached the eighth
floor. He'd covered the distance in record time, and for the
first time in the field he found himself locked in a battle of
willpower with his own mind. He'd heard of the concept of
an adrenalin dump, but he hadn't fully experienced the
sensation until now. The fighting on the ground floor had
sapped him of all his strength, requiring one hundred
percent of his maximum output in the desperate battle for
survival.

Now he fought the urge to sit down and recharge his
internal batteries — there was no time for that. His experiences in the field thus far had been populated by brief, all-
out explosions of violence, with long uninterrupted
stretches of nothingness between them. He had never been
forced to leap from confrontation to confrontation so fast.

You learn something new every time, he thought.

Mustering what little energy he had left, he prepared

himself for what he would find on the eighth floor. Conflict was inevitable, and he steeled himself as he reached the open concrete walkway that the stairwell levelled out onto.

The skyscraper was supposed to spear fifty or sixty storeys into the sky, but construction had ground to a halt on the ninth or tenth floor. Everything above Slater now was nothing but a twisted amalgamation of scaffolding and supports, some of them having already collapsed after months of disuse.

The stairwell had reached its conclusion.

He took a gulp of air, tasting the crisp Chicago night, and then ducked straight through a giant open doorway set into the concrete perimeter wall of the stairwell, leaving the vast vertical tunnel behind. He entered the familiar maze of a half-finished project, skirting around exposed supports and sticking to what little flooring had been erected before the builders had abandoned the site.

At one point he glanced through a grid of steel beams alongside him and blanched at the dizzying drop. Falling through one of the cracks would result in disaster.

Great.

Another thing to seize his attention.

He battled with a wave of conflicting emotions — half of Slater's brain screamed at him to slow down, take his time, approach the situation with focus and discipline, whilst the other half urged him forward, pleading with him to speed up to avoid the risk of the families being murdered before he reached them. If he went too slow, and stumbled across a massacre that he could have prevented, he knew he would never be able to forgive himself.

So he sped up.

Even though it was detrimental to his own safety.

He couldn't allow his own arrival to result in the deaths of all the innocents in the site.

Theresa's estimation ran through his mind. Roughly six or seven hostiles left. Three families, six innocent people total — three women, three children. All wrenched from their homes because of the insider information a bent central district commander had managed to acquire.

D'Agostino, you piece of shit.

Slater heard voices.

Dead ahead.

No time for thought.

Only action.

He raised the Glock, pulse pounding in his ears, heart racing, fatigue seeping in, and powered straight around the corner, ready for anything.

21

They'd heard him coming.

As soon as he burst into the open, rounding the L-shaped bend in the corridor, a blast of air washed against his left cheek. Ordinarily the sensation would mean nothing, but Slater understood exactly what it signified.

A bullet had just come within inches of blowing his face apart.

He recoiled instantly as his own recklessness hammered home. In his last three operations he'd become increasingly brazen with every passing altercation. There was something about being able to react faster than anyone you ran into that made him charge forward with a certain unhinged temperament. Now it had almost cost him his life. Usually he would have rounded the corner and let off a series of shots with the Glock before anyone had even realised he was there, but these men were a class above the common criminal.

Whatever the case, Slater ducked straight back out of sight. Both guys had their weapons trained on the space he'd been occupying a second earlier. Their buddy must have warned them that he was coming.

Heart pounding, he steadied his grip on the Glock and prepared for a close-quarters firefight, something he considered himself excellent at.

But then the two henchmen got greedy, and Slater realised it would be even easier than that.

He heard them barrelling down the hallway toward him not long after he'd ducked out of sight. He figured they were both charging recklessly, probably figuring they could capitalise on his retreat.

Did they really think he was fleeing with his tail between his legs?

They must have expected to send a couple of rounds through his back as he ran away. They hadn't prepared for the fact that Slater was a seasoned professional, and although it might have appeared that he'd turned and run away, he was in fact positioned only a couple of feet around the corner.

So when the first guy — a bulky, six-foot-three Eastern European man with the standard shaved head and sturdy jawline — exploded into sight, Slater put him down with a pair of well-placed shots to the centre mass.

He was a little more accurate, and a little more prepared, than his adversaries.

The twin blasts from the Glock ripped through the top of the construction site, blending with the howling wind seeping through the cracks in the exterior. The first thug dropped like a stone as he took two lead projectiles to the chest, rupturing his internal organs and freezing his mad charge. His legs gave out from underneath him and he started to topple, but not before his friend bringing up the rear of the procession crashed straight into him.

Slater couldn't quite believe his luck.

The second guy tripped over the first and tumbled head over heels across the bend in the corridor. He kept an admirable grip on his weapon — an identical Kalashnikov AK-15 no doubt purchased in bulk from the same supplier — but he didn't get a chance to use it. Slater put a third round straight through the side of the head, taking somewhat more of a risk by targeting the tiny surface area whilst the target was on the move.

But he had momentum on his side.

The shot drilled home.

Both of the gangsters went down in an uncontrollable heap, bleeding from three separate bullet wounds spread across two bodies. Slater didn't spend a moment admiring his handiwork, or even making certain that both hostiles were dead. They were out of commission, and wouldn't pose him any problems, so he instantly forgot about their existence and hustled straight back around the corner, maintaining the same frenetic pace he'd sported earlier.

Because now the bulk of the thugs knew he'd reached the top floor, and they would be prepared to defend their operation with their lives.

Good.

Slater wouldn't give them the chance to surrender anyway.

As he entered a new, unimpressive, half-finished stretch of corridor, he knew immediately where the rest of the gangsters were. He could hear their frantic shouts, the short panicked commands in Russian, and above that the sudden screams of hostages.

Where?

Slater zoned in on a section of the eighth floor that branched off from the hallway he was racing down, spiralling to the right through another unfinished, open doorway. Based on a rough estimate, he figured he was getting close to the front of the construction site. He imagined a wide concrete expanse devoid of furniture or decorations of any kind, exposed to the elements, lacking a roof. He painted a vivid picture of the setting in his mind, because he would need every available millisecond to react once he made it to the final hurdle.

It all came down to this.

Could he perform?

He didn't know. He simply didn't have a clue. The Glock in his palm seemed like an extension of his own body, and his senses had never been more tuned to the present moment, but all the skill in the world couldn't overcome five or six gun barrels pointed in his direction. And he couldn't hesitate — there was almost nothing separating the hostages from death. The thugs would no doubt have a contingency plan in place — eliminate the cumbersome innocents with shots to the head, destroying the collateral, and then flee.

They might be enacting it right now.

So Slater didn't think twice about his own life. He couldn't. Acknowledging the fact that he would have to willingly make the same move that had almost got him killed twenty seconds ago, he raised the Glock to shoulder level and sprinted straight through the open doorway, all the neurons in his brain firing on full alert.

Go time.

22

The first incoming shot hit him in the soft flesh on top of his left hand.

In fact, it didn't sink home. It simply grazed past, taking most of the skin off in a thin line, sending specks of blood flying back into Slater's own eyes. Despite the screaming nerve endings and the sudden hot burst of agony and the shock to his system as he realised he'd been hit, he kept his composure. Eyes darting in ten directions at once, he surveyed the scene at the same time as the bullet sliced across his hand and passed him by.

The expanse certainly was concrete, and it certainly was devoid of furniture or obstacles of any kind, and it certainly didn't have a roof — all the things he'd conjured up in his mind's eye before entering the room. It was a giant grey bowl, with half-completed walls and a couple of empty rectangular holes in the far wall looking out over the urban Chicago street. Construction had ceased before window panes had been put into place. Wild activity was taking place in every corner of the room at once — burly men hauled small children and cowering women off the dusty floor, urging them to their feet as fast as they could, preparing them for movement.

Too late.

Slater had arrived.

He counted five remaining men at first glance, all carbon copies of each other. It made sense — living in squalor amidst an ageing construction site, they probably employed the same daily routines. All five of them were pale-skinned and sported identical buzzcuts. They were all built like tanks, either a byproduct of their profession or an attempt to stay in shape whilst laying low. They all seemed to originate from the same region — inductive reasoning pegged them as Eastern European, considering everyone he'd dealt with so far sported the same ethnicity. Even from a single glance he could see coldness in their demeanours — these were harsh, cruel men, accustomed to fighting for survival and making a living however they could. They would have served D'Agostino well, and none of them would understand the concept of surrender.

They wouldn't even consider it.

Slater weighed all this up in a split second. Next he assessed the nearest hostiles — he quickly determined that the man who'd shot him was the same guy whose nose Slater had shattered downstairs.

In the carnage, Slater had almost forgotten the fact that his own nose was broken, too.

This man was the closest, and his Heckler & Koch sidearm was raised to shoulder height in anticipation for Slater's arrival. As far as Slater could tell, none of the other four thugs had bothered to line their aim up with the open doorway. They all had bulky rifles swinging off shoulder straps, but they were uniformly preoccupied with the hostages.

Done.

Situation processed.

All in the time it took for blood to spray off Slater's hand and into his eyes.

Black Force recruited those with phenomenal reaction speeds for a reason.

Because in situations like these, when the odds were horrifically stacked against Slater, he could still come out on top.

He turned and blasted two shots in the direction of the guy with the broken nose. Both struck home, punching twin holes in the man's forehead, and the guy folded over unnaturally as important neural connections were destroyed by lead. Slater ignored him, deploying a mental tally mark to indicate a neutralised enemy, and maintained his mad pace deeper into the room.

Now, two of the remaining four started to react to the gunshots. Slater was locked in a tunnel, zoned in on anything that lay in front of him with zero regard for any other aspect of his consciousness. He'd experienced the feeling a couple of times before, and it was difficult to properly articulate how everything clicked, but he transitioned seamlessly from one millisecond to another in a way he couldn't understand. Everything was streamlined. All the stars were aligned.

He was ready.

Ignoring the blood pumping out of his left hand — he barely even noticed the injury had happened, and perhaps wouldn't have realised at all if not for his own blood spraying across his face — he wrenched the Glock's aim from hostile to hostile, laser-focusing on the two men raising assault rifles in his direction. With barrels heading his way, he knew he could fire at will without any risk of wild shots hitting the hostages. If the two thugs were going to impulsively pull their triggers in their death throes, the bullets would hit Slater instead of the hostages.

That suited him just fine.

So he hit the guy on the left twice in the chest, and sent a third round through the throat of the guy on the right. All three bullets did obscene damage, and they sunk home before either of the pair had the chance to fire a shot. The rapidity with which events were unfolding, coupled with Slater's constant movement and complete lack of hesitation, resulted in a strange, dream-like experience for the hostiles. They would have barely registered Slater's presence before he fired rounds into them and dropped them where they stood.

Which was exactly what happened to the pair he targeted.

They collapsed — one of the gangsters crumpled into the side of the kid he'd been pulling to his feet, a small boy no older than eight. The child screamed and jerked away from the body, wrapping his tiny arms around his mother standing only a foot behind him.

Slater couldn't pay the situation any attention.

He couldn't afford to waste a millisecond.

Two left.

It was strange to even attempt to process what was happening. Slater knew he was moving, and he knew his life was on the line, but the speed with which he had to react took its toll, transitioning him over to an impulsive, reactionary state he couldn't control. He relied on the years of constant training and discipline to carry him through. He simply isolated the next targets, and surged toward them.

Too late.

He saw the gun arcing in his direction, but this time

even his unfathomable reflexes couldn't save him. The big Eastern European man behind the Kalashnikov was going to let off a couple of shots, and Slater's charge into the room had taken him directly into the line of fire. He had sprinted forward with such brazenness that he ended up only a few feet away from the big man when the muzzle of the Kalashnikov flared and bullets spat from the rifle.

Pain seared through Slater.

He'd been directly hit.

23

He didn't have time to discern the damage.

In that moment in time all other thoughts fell away, replaced by the sheer instinct to survive. He zigzagged from left to right like a madman, putting all his momentum and energy into acting as wild as possible, but even the most efficient movements couldn't dodge bullets. The thug would manage roughly three or four shots by the time Slater closed the gap and surged out of the line of fire.

He needed to survive for the next half-second, and prevent himself from succumbing to any life-threatening injuries.

Which proved harder than he originally anticipated.

The rifle cracked four times, shockingly close, aimed right in Slater's direction. Pain exploded in his hand holding the Glock, and the weapon fell out of his hands as blood spurted. He didn't have time to check where he'd been hit, because another round grazed his hip, running a thin red line across the side of his jeans. The third must have missed, because Slater didn't feel any hot burst of fire, and the fourth came within an inch of his throat. Any kind of connection with that sensitive area would have left him bleeding out on the floor, but by the time he hurled himself into the man with every last ounce of effort in his body, he found himself flabbergasted that he was still alert and breathing.

Bleeding, sure, but alive.

The two spilled to the ground and Slater descended into a rage, tapping into the natural high that came from surviving a situation he'd considered unsalvageable. He'd fully expected to take four rounds to the chest or head and find his synapses cut off as he sunk into an early grave, but the thug must have been jittery with his aim and missed the bulk of his shots. Slater caught a fleeting glimpse of his right hand and saw blood flowing from the webbing between his thumb and index finger — the bullet had torn straight through the skin. With both his hands mangled, he had no hope of using them to throw punches.

But he didn't need his fists to finish a fight.

He drove a knee down into the guy's stomach, pinning him against the dusty concrete, and smashed the Kalashnikov out of his grip with a side-swiping elbow. The rifle skittered away, now useless, and Slater changed direction with the same elbow and dropped it into the thug's unprotected face. Red hot anger took over and Slater used the shift in momentum to deliver another elbow, then another, then another, pumping his left arm like a piston until the man underneath him offered no more resistance.

He wasn't dead, but Slater had smashed him unconscious in the space of a couple of seconds, no thanks to the burning intensity running through his veins.

The thug had come within an inch of ending Slater's life.

That deserved retaliation.

Slater fell off the thug. Pain seared in his hip, and his hands throbbed uncontrollably, but he didn't pay any of his injuries a sliver of attention. They were superficial, and they meant nothing in the grand scheme of things. What mattered above all else was the last remaining hostile in the room, the sole guy up the back of the concrete box that Slater had glimpsed earlier. Slater's vision was a blur but he rolled like a madman toward the loaded Kalashnikov, wondering how the hell he was going to fire the gun with a pair of hands that had suffered grievous injuries.

He didn't have time to think about it.

At any moment, he expected to catch a bullet as he moved. He vaguely sensed cowering innocents all around him, pressed up against each of the respective walls with their heads bowed as chaos raged in the room, but Slater couldn't spot the last guy anywhere. Admittedly, he hadn't stopped to look yet, madly scrambling for the dormant rifle he'd elbowed away, but the guy could be anywhere.

Slater clamped a bloody hand down on the Kalashnikov and finally took the time to dart his vision around the room, searching for any sign of...

No shots came. No bullets struck the dusty ground around him, or punched straight through his clothing and sunk into his flesh. He heard no crack of automatic weaponry, or even so much as a string of Russian cursing.

In fact, he couldn't have heard a thing if he tried.

The four shots the last thug had fired from the AK-15 had effectively deafened Slater. Besides the fact that most of them had grazed him, they had burst from the barrel of the rifle at such close proximity that his eardrums might have been permanently disabled. He could hear nothing over the heartbeat pounding in his ears.

But where the hell is the last guy?

Then, in the tunnel vision that had settled over him, he saw it.

The cluster of three people, their backs turned to Slater, fleeing at breakneck speed from the room.

Hustling straight through the same doorway he'd entered moments earlier.

The last thug, barrel-chested and broad-shouldered, with big pasty hands the size of dustbin lids, had a frail thirty-something woman with brunette hair and a young girl no older than ten in a vice-like grip, holding them by an arm each. With both hands preoccupied, the assault rifle on a shoulder strap was swinging uselessly across his burly frame. He didn't have the resources to use it.

But he didn't need to.

He was fleeing with his precious cargo.

Slater only caught a glimpse of the trio, and by the time he brought his own weapon up to aim at the doorway, they had vanished.

24

T*he gun.*
His brain switched over to autopilot.
Get the goddamn gun, and move.

He reached down and snatched at the Kalashnikov, wrapping one hand around the stock and one hand around the grip. He wrenched it off the ground. Crimson blood ran slick between his fingers and the cold steel of the weapon, and the rifle slipped from his grasp. It clattered back to the dust.

One second ticked by.

Veins straining in his forehead, Slater made another wild grab for the rifle. Pain tore through both his hands, blood flowing from the pair of wounds. Neither bullet had lodged in his hand, but the skin had been shredded all the same. Grimacing, he wrenched the AK-15 off the ground.

It slipped again.

Another second ticked by.

You don't have time.

You can't grip anything.

You need to move.

The primal, instinctual part of his brain that was permanently set to fight-or-flight begged him to stay where he was. It pleaded with his common sense, demanding that he was too injured to continue. Any kind of pursuit he could make would only result in his own demise. There was no point. He was already woozy from blood loss, and he had no idea how badly the bullet had cut his hip. For all he knew, he could only have seconds of consciousness left.

So he stayed on one knee for the briefest of moments in time. He looked around, spotting the two separate families on either side of the giant space. Both mothers were cradling their children against their chests, protecting them from any further harm.

And the last remaining thug had just run off with the final pair.

Slater clenched his teeth. He couldn't do it. He couldn't stay put. It went against everything he stood for, everything he'd worked toward over the course of his career.

He had to move.

Even if it resulted in his own death.

He made one last snatch for the gun, and again it slipped — this time he barely got his fingers around the Kalashnikov before crippling agony arced up his wrist and made him involuntarily let go of the rifle.

Useless.

He couldn't grip anything.

Go.

Unarmed, reeling from the chaos, he took off at a flat out sprint across the space, surging after the trio that had fled the room seconds earlier. He couldn't quite fathom how he was even standing, but he somehow managed. He was a twenty-three year old athlete in his prime, and the big Eastern European brute would be burdened by the two resisting hostages he was dragging along with him.

That was enough to convince Slater that he had a chance of catching them.

But then what?

The guy had a rifle, and Slater had nothing. He couldn't even use his hands.

Cross that bridge when you come to it.

So he pushed himself faster. He raced back out into the corridor and turned left, pumping his arms and legs like pistons. Blood dripped off his hands but he ignored it. He covered distance as fast as his legs would allow, battling down the natural urge to stop and tend to his injuries. He didn't have time to do anything but put one foot in front of the other and barrel toward his target.

It was the only way he'd ever done things.

If he came across the trio and slowed down, he would die. He had nothing to defend himself with except his own body, and he couldn't use that unless he closed the gap between himself and the last thug in record time. He wouldn't get lucky twice — if the thug had a beat on him with the Kalashnikov, it would only take one squeeze of the trigger in such a confined space to finish Slater off.

He had to hope for a miracle.

He had to hope the thug would be distracted.

He reached the entrance to the giant stairwell, and even from a distance he could see the vast vertical tunnel lay shrouded in shadow. It would be close to four in the morning, if Slater's calculations were accurate, and the night pressed down on everything. It helped him forget what kind of state he was in — it was hard to notice the blood in the darkness.

Slater heard motion — the sounds of struggle — coming through the open doorway to the stairwell. He didn't think twice.

He hurried straight through.

25

S later sprinted out onto the same concrete platform as before, facing the same precipitous drop that speared eight storeys down through the centre of the stairwell, culminating at the ground floor. With no central partition to split up the stairs, the descent to the ground floor consisted of the concrete spiral arcing around the perimeter walls, heading down into the darkness.

Directly ahead, the trio were ready to descend.

Slater could barely make out their silhouettes in the lowlight. Above his head, the night sky hung overbearing and grim, providing the slightest natural illumination. He'd caught the thug at the final hurdle — the man was wrestling with the woman and the child, who were doing everything they could feasibly manage to break free. He had them both by the arms, hurrying them toward the first flight of stairs, dangerously close to the unobstructed edge of the eighth storey platform.

If they struggled too hard, either of the hostages might take a step too far to the right and plummet to their deaths. There was threadbare scaffolding and steel supports intersecting across the central drop, but it wouldn't be enough to break their falls.

If they did manage to crash to a halt amidst one of the erected wooden platforms, it would result in such a shocking list of injuries that death would be inevitable.

Slater slowed his pace.

He had to.

He couldn't immediately work out which of the silhouettes was the thug. The child was immediately recognisable as a young girl, tiny in comparison to the other two, but even though the woman and the giant gangster were vastly different sizes, it was still hard to fathom in the dark. It took a vital half-second to deduce who the enemy was — the last thing Slater wanted to do was target the wrong outline.

He got his target sorted, and broke into an all-out sprint.

There was less than ten feet between them.

Then everything changed.

Almost in slow motion, Slater spotted the thug's head twist as the man looked over his shoulder. In the darkness the pair locked eyes as best they could, and Slater saw recognition spread across the man's face.

He knew Slater was coming for him.

The dynamic shifted.

The guy immediately stopped trying to wrestle with the hostages. Slater could almost tell what he was thinking. This mysterious dark-skinned intruder had mown through their entire force, decimating them with apparent ease. The thug didn't know how hurt Slater was.

He must have imagined his own time was up, his death inevitable at the hands of this phenom.

But one thing was certain. Slater was desperate to protect the hostages.

And that was the one minuscule victory the thug could seize before he died.

He could strip Slater of his success. He could tear the one thing away from him that he valued above anything else.

The protection of the woman and her child.

Slater sensed all of this in a heartbeat, but there was nothing he could do to stop it. He was already sprinting full pelt toward the trio — there was no way to increase his pace, nothing that shouting a warning would achieve. He saw the thug reach down and gather up the Kalashnikov AK-15 swinging from the strap on his hip, but instead of trying to point it in Slater's direction he sent the barrel scything upward to aim at the pair of hostages.

Just like that, everything became clear.

Slater knew what he needed to do.

He couldn't slow down. If he had any hope of succeeding at the last second, he would need to sprint directly into the side of the thug, which would send both of them tumbling off the side of the enormous stairwell with uncontrollable momentum. He would need to carry them both into the abyss, falling eight storeys through a mountain of scaffolding to their deaths.

Did he have it in him to sacrifice himself, right here and right now?

Could he do that?

It didn't matter.

Even turning his mind to the question made him hesitate, so imperceptible and unnoticeable that no-one would have ever known that he slowed down, even if they'd been staring directly at him.

But he knew.

Deep in his mind, he knew that he slowed.

He was *going* to commit. He told himself that. He accepted the fact that he would die for this woman and this child that he'd never met. He knew he had that capacity, and he barrelled straight onward.

But that split second of questioning, that tiny shred of time in which he had to ponder whether he could...

...that was all it took.

The thug pulled the trigger of the Kalashnikov before Slater could reach him. He was only a couple of feet away by that point, but the muzzle flare burst into life all the same, and the bullet left the barrel all the same, and the frail woman no older than thirty-five crumpled all the same.

Lifeless.

Unmoving.

Dead.

Slater's insides melted. Crippling anguish rolled through him, even as he continued his feverish pace toward the thug.

Now they were a foot apart.

Half a foot.

The thug swung the aim of the Kalashnikov around to aim at the young girl, the barrel slicing through the air to line up with her head.

She screamed, a piercing shrill that cut through the night and echoed down the stairwell.

No.

Slater knew what he had to do.

This time, he didn't slow down for a millisecond.

He ran into the side of the thug at close to the speed of an Olympic sprinter, crash-tackling the guy with enough bone-crushing momentum to send them both sprawling off their feet, carried through the air and over the edge of the precipice. The impact rattled Slater's brain inside his skull and he gave thanks to the semi-conscious state he slumped into as he used his own body as a battering ram.

Together, they plunged into the darkness.

And the gun hadn't gone off a second time.

26

For what seemed like forever, Slater felt weightless. His stomach sunk into his feet, overriding all the superficial pain racing through him. He lost touch with the thug and the bulky Eastern European man spiralled away in the darkness, crashing into a mass of scaffolding with enough of a sickening *squelch* for Slater to recognise the guy as unquestionably dead.

Then there was just his own fate to worry about.

He didn't imagine he would have to worry for much longer.

Half a second later he smashed into a wooden platform with enough force to splinter it into two massive pieces. He tore straight through, letting out an unbridled yell as he sensed the bone in his forearm snap cleanly in two. He fell another few feet and bounced off a metal pipe, knocked off-course into another mess of plastic sheeting and wooden planks. This time he crunched through enough material to slow him considerably, and when he finally came to a halt amidst the devastation it took him a few beats to realise he was alive.

Probably not for long.

He'd never experienced pain quite like this. Battlefield injuries could be gruesome, but they seldom carried the intensity of what he was feeling right now. A bullet wound resulting in massive blood loss could cause unconsciousness pretty fast, but this was a different kind of injury. Blunt force trauma had been applied to every square inch of his body, and he realised the extent of his wounds when he tried to shift his weight around in the pile of wood and rubble and found himself helpless.

He couldn't move.

The headache that surged into existence drilled into his eyeballs, like a blowtorch applied to his brain. He could barely stomach the agony, and when his vision transitioned into murky darkness he almost welcomed it. Anything would be a relief compared to the beating his body had taken from the fall. Then again, the fact that was he alive to feel this pain was a pleasant surprise. He'd been ready to die when he hurled himself off the edge of the eighth floor, and that knowledge would take some time to process when he regained his health.

The darkness was absolute, and Slater could see nothing. He didn't even know where he'd come to rest — it couldn't have been much lower than the sixth floor, considering a longer fall would almost certainly have killed him. He lay motionless, surrounded by destruction, and waited for something, anything, to happen.

At some point he blacked out. Amidst the cocktail of pain wracking his body and the darkened surroundings on all sides, it was hard to tell when unconsciousness took hold. Everything was a seething blur of swirling night. His awareness became similar to an old projector switching between slides — every now and then something happened to seize his attention. A flash of light. A quiet voice. Some kind of commotion nearby. None of it meant anything. If there were any members of the Eastern European gang left in the construction site, they would dispose of him fairly effortlessly. He couldn't move.

Although getting him out of the scaffolding would prove cumbersome.

He kept lying there, and hurting, and exhaling laboured breaths. He couldn't do anything else. Hours seemed to pass, but it might have been minutes.

When the broken scaffolding around him started to move, and the whir of some kind of heavy machinery started up close by, he could barely muster the energy to turn his head. It seemed as if he'd aged ten years, but that didn't make any sense considering it was still dark.

A blinding light shone in his face, and the wooden planks underneath him shifted in place — the entire framework of scaffolding he was resting on had been adjusted. More machinery whined, and a calm voice asked him if he was okay.

He wasn't sure where the words came from.

He couldn't see what lay inches in front of his face.

He nodded once, and then blacked out again.

Sinking to a darker place.

Before he fully gave himself over to the darkness, he played back the mental image of the woman's body crumpling on the eighth floor. He thought of the way her shoulders had slumped, and her knees had given out, and all the life had been sapped from her in an inconceivably short amount of time.

He would never forget it.

27

Thirty days later...

L ars Crawford didn't particularly like Chicago all that much.

He kept a purposeful stride through the downtown district, never losing sight of the destination he had in mind. Every now and then he locked eyes with the odd passerby, and he never failed to exchange a polite nod of acknowledgement with them. By all accounts he was a quiet, unassuming man. He wondered if anyone would guess that during work hours — which seemed to consist of every waking moment these days — he ran one of the most secretive government divisions the United States military had ever seen.

At five-foot-nine, with a skinny unathletic frame and a weak jawline, he didn't have much in common with most of the black operations soldiers he handled on a day to day basis. By necessity, they were often large, unimaginably powerful men with the physical capabilities to effectively carry out the instructions delivered to them by their own brilliant minds.

Prodigies, all things considered.

Lars certainly labelled Will Slater a prodigy.

In the aftermath of the destruction, it had been concluded that Slater had killed thirteen men — Ray D'Agostino included — on that single night in Chicago. Of course, none of this had been officially determined by any authorities — Black Force had their own internal investigation process, something of a requirement when they controlled operatives who could do whatever the hell they wanted in the field. They needed to hold their men accountable for their actions, and after a turbulent two weeks of consideration, Lars and his superiors had come to the conclusion that Will Slater had done incredible work.

An unsavoury collection of Dagestani criminals had been massacred, and the police and media had chalked it up to a horrific gang war. No-one had ever suspected it had been the work of a single individual.

An individual who Lars had flown from Washington to meet.

He'd already been given the address. He found the rusting metal door wedged between a delicatessen and a barber, sporting a tiny silver plaque with the inscription *LIONEL'S BOXING GYM* carved in uneven letters. Not his first choice for their first in-person meeting since the debacle had unfolded, but Slater was the one calling the shots.

He could afford to now, after everything he'd done.

Lars and his colleagues all understood the intrinsic value they had in an operative like Will Slater.

Even though he was young, he was walking in the foot-steps of the warrior responsible for the division's creation.

For the first time ever, Lars found himself thinking, *Jason King's got competition.*

He descended a narrow set of concrete stairs, battling a small wave of claustrophobia. The ceiling hovered only a few inches above his head, and the confines of the space stank of dried sweat and exertion. Lars was unsurprised that Slater had ended up here, especially considering the fact that doctors had told him it would take six months to get back to full health.

At five thirty in the morning, Slater was the only man here. Apparently he'd struck up a relationship with the owner over the course of his month-long recuperation, and the elderly Lionel allowed Slater twenty-four-seven access to the space. Lars had taken the information in stride, simply nodding when one of his underlings informed him about the odd development.

Slater's physical condition wasn't the only thing the man needed to recuperate.

Lars found Slater in the corner of the gym, which consisted of a long low stretch of basement with memorabilia on the walls and old-school boxing equipment spread across the floor. The man had taken up position in front of a heavy bag shaped like a teardrop, suspended from the concrete ceiling by a thick metal chain.

Old-school.

Just the way Slater liked it.

Lars crossed the room, overwhelmingly out of place amongst the sweat-stained equipment, and kept his mouth shut as he observed one of his finest operatives. Slater stood with his chin held high, possessed with an inner confidence, refusing to cower in the face of the list of injuries he'd suffered. Some obstacles couldn't be overcome, so his left arm remained bound in a sling as the bones in his forearm healed from a pair of clean breaks.

But his right arm worked just fine.

An eight-ounce boxing glove had been pulled over Slater's right fist, covered in sweat droplets that had run down his arm. The man was shirtless, wearing simple athletic shorts, and as Lars watched he hammered a relentless stream of uppercuts into the heavy bag, shouting with every impact. Sweat sprayed off his frame with every blow. There wasn't an ounce of body fat on him, even though he'd been bed ridden for close to a month. Lars could see the spark in his eyes, the feverish rage spurring him onward. He counted twenty-eight consecutive uppercuts before Slater dropped his one-armed attack and took a deep breath, allowing the perspiration to cascade off him in droves.

'You sleeping?' Lars said, leaning against one post of the nearby boxing ring.

Slater turned, running the glove over his forehead to wipe away the sweat. 'Not really. I just see her crumpling. Over and over again.'

Lars nodded.

The woman, Brooke Davies, had been thirty-two years old. The bullet had struck her in the centre of her chest and pulverised her internal organs. There had been no chance of survival. Her daughter had seen everything, and was being monitored for signs of post-traumatic stress disorder. She was back home with her father.

'You did unbelievable work, Will,' Lars said. 'You can't forget that.'

Slater stood motionless for a long beat, then turned and hammered another uppercut into the heavy bag. The sound of the leather glove hitting the material sent a gunshot-like *crack* through the empty basement.

'I did work,' he said. 'It wasn't unbelievable. She died.'

'You saved seven people.'

'I should have saved eight.'

'Slater...'

'When am I back in the field?'

'Uh...'

'Surely you have something lined up?'

'Your arm, Will.'

'It's healing. As soon as it's ready, I want something.'

'An operation?'

'The worst shit you've got.'

'We have a lot of bad stuff. That's sort of the nature of this job.'

'I don't care where you send me. But get me moving again.'

'You want to make things right?'

'Of course. Only way I can do that is to succeed next time.'

'You succeeded this time.'

'No, I didn't.'

'Four kids who got to go home to their families will tell you otherwise.'

'Brooke's not here to tell me anything.'

'What happened in that construction site, Slater?'

Lars was desperate for genuine information. Slater had been frustratingly quiet about the entire ordeal, withdrawing into himself as soon as he was able to recover in private. There had been the painstaking process of withdrawing him from the public hospital system after the authorities had pried him out of the stairwell one month earlier, but as soon as Black Force had silenced anyone in the know and calmly informed the necessary parties that Slater no longer existed, he'd been free to recover in privacy.

And he hadn't felt like talking much at all.

Slater twisted on the spot again, revealing glistening muscles trailing up his abdomen, and smashed another punch into the heavy bag with lethal ferocity. If he'd been targeting a human being, he might have killed them from the blunt force trauma alone.

'I hesitated,' he said.

'Froze on the spot?'

'Sort of. You wouldn't have been able to tell. But I did.'

'And you think you could've saved Brooke otherwise?'

'I know I could've.'

'So what happens now? How's your headspace?'

Three more punches detonated off the leather bag.

Bang.

Bang.

Bang.

'Headspace is fine,' Slater muttered. 'But get me back out there as soon as you can.'

'To do what?'

Slater stared at Lars across the room, a bright glint in his eyes. 'Not hesitate.'

'I'll see what I can do,' Lars mumbled. 'Take it easy, hey? You don't want to disrupt the healing process of that arm.'

'I am taking it easy,' Slater said, and fired off two punches into the bag, veins pumping and sweat flowing.

Lars nodded, and turned his back on Will Slater.

Making his way up to the downtown Chicago street, he found himself intensely curious to see what Slater did next. Something told him he had his hands on one of the most notable raw talents the military had ever seen. Not for his physical gifts, or his mental prowess — there were dozens of prodigies that had come through the ranks of the Special Forces over the years.

But when Lars found someone with that type of relentless mindset, he didn't take it lightly.

A soft voice in the back of his head told him Will Slater would have a career for the ages.

MORE BLACK FORCE SHORTS COMING VERY SOON...

Follow Slater's post-military career with the following
action-thrillers:

THE WILL SLATER SERIES
Wolf (Book 1)
Lion (Book 2)

Visit amazon.com/author/mattrogers23 and press **"Follow"**
to be automatically notified of my future releases.

If you enjoyed the hard-hitting adventure, make sure to
leave a review! Your feedback means everything to me, and
encourages me to deliver more Black Force thrillers as soon
as I can.

Stay tuned.

Join the Reader's Group and get a free 200-page book by Matt Rogers!

Sign up for a free copy of '**HARD IMPACT**'.
Meet Jason King — another member of Black Force.

Experience King's most dangerous mission — action-packed insanity in the heart of the Amazon Rainforest.

No spam guaranteed.

Just click here.

BOOKS BY MATT ROGERS

THE JASON KING SERIES

Isolated (Book 1)

Imprisoned (Book 2)

Reloaded (Book 3)

Betrayed (Book 4)

Corrupted (Book 5)

Hunted (Book 6)

THE JASON KING FILES

Cartel (Book 1)

Warrior (Book 2)

Savages (Book 3)

THE WILL SLATER SERIES

Wolf (Book 1)

Lion (Book 2)

BLACK FORCE SHORTS

The Victor (Book 1)

The Chimera (Book 2)

The Tribe (Book 3)

The Hidden (Book 4)

ABOUT THE AUTHOR

Matt Rogers grew up in Melbourne, Australia as a voracious reader, relentlessly devouring thrillers and mysteries in his spare time. Now, he writes full-time. His novels are action-packed and fast-paced. Dive into the Jason King Series to get started with his collection.

Visit his website:

www.mattrogersbooks.com

Visit his Amazon page:

amazon.com/author/mattrogers23

Printed in Great Britain
by Amazon